Dear Reader,

For those of you who hav~~e~~ ... you might
have noticed that I love food. My characters all share
my food obsessions—they find comfort in chocolate
and peanut butter, they recognize the beauty of
bacon and they know that a Mi Fiesta burrito really
is the perfect food. I know that this isn't a healthy
obsession. I have tried to cultivate the same feelings
for carrots and apples, but frankly, they just aren't
as delicious.

For me, part of loving food comes from cooking
and I learned from some great cooks over the years
working as a waitress and prep cook. Those jobs
also gave me a front-row seat for the theatrics of
a professional kitchen. The romances, egos and
creativity—there was never a dull moment. The
seed for this story was born watching behind the
scenes of a good brunch rush.

Since all the chefs I have known are passionate,
creative and driven people and sparks always fly when
they fall in love, *Dishing It Out* made perfect sense.
Sparks certainly fly between Van MacAllister, my half-
Scottish, half-Italian chef, and Marie Simmons—Anna's
sister from *Pencil Him In*, Flipside #15—a woman with
a small, but growing, cooking empire to protect.
I hope you enjoy their story!

Check out my Web site at www.molly-okeefe.com.
You'll find some of the recipes Van and Marie make in
the book. And please share some of your favorites!

Happy reading,

Molly O'Keefe

"Look who's on the cover of the Weekend Magazine."

Marie looked at the magazine her producer Simon held up. Van MacAllister was staring at her in full-color, glossy arrogance.

"That's great," she lied, feeling certain she sounded convincing. "Good for him." She tried to ignore the giant spike of irritation she always felt about Van. With his new restaurant across the street from her own, he had single-handedly made the past six months of her life even more strained and tiring.

"You're not still upset about what he said in the *Examiner*, are you?" Simon asked.

"I'm not upset." She shrugged and unclenched her fists. She'd sworn she wouldn't wallow in her anger over him. "I mean, just because he called my bistro a 'cute little coffee shop' in an international paper, why would I be upset?" Marie felt a rant approaching and knew she had to stop before she scared Simon. "So why are we talking about Van?"

"This is big, Marie. Exciting." Simon paused to grin outrageously. "Meet your new cohost!"

Dishing It Out

Molly O'Keefe

Grandma Lucy!
A mean Bingo Player!
Thanks so much
Molly O'Keefe

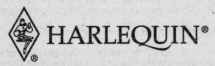

HARLEQUIN®

TORONTO • NEW YORK • LONDON
AMSTERDAM • PARIS • SYDNEY • HAMBURG
STOCKHOLM • ATHENS • TOKYO • MILAN • MADRID
PRAGUE • WARSAW • BUDAPEST • AUCKLAND

ISBN 0-373-44211-4

DISHING IT OUT

ABOUT THE AUTHOR

Molly O'Keefe grew up reading in a small farming town outside of Chicago. She went to Webster University in St. Louis where she graduated with a degree in Journalism and English and met a Canadian who became her college editor, and later her husband and tennis partner. She spent a year writing for regional publications and St. Louis newspapers, before she began moving around the country and writing romance novels. At age 25, she sold her first book to Harlequin Duets, got married and settled down in Toronto, Canada. She and her husband share a cat and dreams of warmer climates.

Books by Molly O'Keefe

HARLEQUIN FLIPSIDE
15—PENCIL HIM IN

HARLEQUIN DUETS
62—TOO MANY COOKS
95—COOKING UP TROUBLE/
    KISS THE COOK

To Sinead, Maureen, Mary, Michele, Susan and Teresa for the advice, food, booze, ideas, laughs, sympathetic ears and constant, steady and crucial support. You make this process a joy. I can't thank you enough, ladies.

1

"CHOCOLATE IS SEXY," Marie Simmons said, smiling into the eye of the camera. "It should taste good, smell good and yes—" she spooned berry coulis over the top of a gorgeous flourless chocolate cake "—feel good. Remind you of anything?" She arched an eyebrow and the studio audience laughed, giving her a few moments to stall. She shot the camera a smile and then scanned her workspace for the mint while she blathered on about sexy food. *Mint!* There it was, under the bowl of raspberries. She broke off some leaves and pressed it into the cake's fudgy soft center.

Running out of time, she told herself. She'd have to scrap the homemade whipped cream, though it was gorgeous.

She lifted the warm cake, tilting it toward the audience and the camera. She smiled in what she hoped was a cool and confident manner. "Good food doesn't just feed the body, it feeds the soul."

She winked and the crowd cheered.

Martha Stewart ain't got nothing on me! Marie

howled inside of her head. She managed to keep herself from doing victory laps around the stage. Another great and mostly disaster-free segment of *Soul Food* done.

Marie caught sight of the floor manager, Roger, in the shadows past the lights, frantically gesturing for Marie to tilt the chocolate fondant up more so the camera could have a better angle. "Up," he mouthed, lifting his hands in slow motion.

She shook her head. Any more angling and the cake would be all over the floor. But Roger was getting red in the face so she tilted the plate and hoped it would stick until the cameras were off.

I finally get a segment with no fires, short circuits, broken dishes or blood and I am going to ruin it by dropping a cake on the floor.

Roger yelled, "Cut!" and Marie sighed, putting the plate back on the counter. The miniature kitchen set that *Soul Food* called home was suddenly swarmed with men and women dressed in black, wearing little headsets. They had ninety seconds to clean her set, break it down and get it out of the way for the rest of the live morning show.

There was so little time or room for error. It reminded Marie of being in a kitchen during a dinner rush. Live TV was like jumping out of a plane, and sometimes *cooking* on live TV was like jumping out of a plane with a possibly faulty parachute.

Marie unhooked her mic, took off her apron and ran backstage, getting out of the crew's way.

Her segment producer and good friend, Simon, was waiting for her in the wings with a bottle of water and a giant grin.

"Great show, Marie!" he whispered.

"Thank you, Mr. Producer," she said and, feeling a huge gust of affection for him, bent down to kiss his shiny bald head.

Good old Simon. Six months ago he turned his addiction to her lemon bars and lentil salad into a monthly gig on *AMSF*, the most popular morning show in the Bay Area. Three months ago, they gave her another half-hour slot and now she was on twice a month.

"Coming through!" A woman carrying a giant cat for the next segment came running past them.

Showbiz, Marie decided, *is definitely for me.*

She felt alive here, fully on top of her game. She didn't feel like she was pretending under those bright lights. Even when things went wrong, like the grease fire two weeks ago, she felt in charge and in control. If not a little singed.

Almost unconsciously, she touched one of the bracelets she wore on her wrists, tracing the moons that were pressed into the silver. The bracelets were reminders of the lessons she had learned from those times she got more than a little singed by the choices she had made.

The music soared and the lights came up on the main stage where the hosts of *AMSF* were sitting at their desk.

"That woman could make popcorn sexy," Rick Anderson, one of the hosts and general all around sleazebag, said, shaking his head. "I think I'm in love."

Marie rolled her eyes at Simon.

"Well, her food is delicious," Luanne, the other host, said in agreement. "That cake looked amazing." The crowd made sounds of approval and Marie felt as if her feet had actually lifted off the ground.

I wonder if I can get a dressing room? Something with a star.

"Let's go up to my office," Simon whispered next to her ear. "I have something I want to talk to you about." Marie nodded and followed him through the backstage maze, up some stairs to his small crowded office with a view of the parking lot two floors below.

Simon's messy desk dominated the office and a bulletin board covered in colored index cards represented the different segments Simon produced for *AMSF. Soul Food* was yellow. She smiled and flicked one with her finger as she walked by.

"The show is popular, Marie. Very, very popular." He smiled at her as he crossed the room to his chair.

"Good," Marie said expansively. "Great!" She was a little in love with the world right now. Drunk with the taste of success. "That's what you pay me the big bucks for." *Ha! Nothing funnier than jokes about being broke.* Maybe if she made enough of them, Simon would get the hint and give her a raise.

She slid into one of the hard wooden seats across from his desk and smothered a yawn, fighting the exhaustion that was crowding the edges of her adrenaline high. *What I wouldn't give for about a gallon of coffee.*

"How's business?" Simon asked, disregarding her joke.

Marie started to take out the bobby pins that Hair and Makeup insisted she wear to keep her black curls out of the food. She was as hygienic as the next chef, but these bobby pins *hurt*. "Since *Soul Food* started going twice a month, brunches are lined up out the door on weekends and we've really picked up lunch hours. It couldn't be better."

Well, that was a lie, but Simon didn't need to know about the girl she hired who had been skimming the till for three weeks. He also didn't need to know about the broken dishwasher.

"You finally getting some sleep since you hired the new baker?"

"He quit." Simon really didn't need to know about that.

"Quit? But that guy was so excited." Simon looked like a little dog when he was surprised. It was cute.

"Apparently, being a baker is exciting in theory but not so much in practice at three in the morn-

ing." Marie shook out the bun her hair had been
pressure-formed into and sighed happily.

Marie could have told the kid that baking
wasn't exactly exciting but she had just been
happy to get another baker in the door. *Nothing
ventured, nothing gained, or something like that.*
"What can you do?"

"So you're still doing it yourself?" Simon
looked sympathetic as he sat down in front of his
large window and leaned back in his seat. He
probably hadn't seen 3:00 a.m. in years, if ever. She
knew he had to get up early for the show. But 5:00
a.m. was not 3:00 a.m. It was an ugly hour, and
Marie had been getting to know it intimately for
the last year.

"I am. You want to volunteer?" she asked, trying to keep things light. "We could tape it for the
show. I think viewers would like to see my producer make scones." Between Ariel the thief, the
dishwasher on the fritz, her organic milk guy dou-
bling his rates and the sleepless nights she'd been
having lately, it was either keep things light or get
dehydrated from all the bawling.

"Not on your life," Simon laughed.

"That's what everyone says." Marie tried to
push the sleeve of her deep purple chenille
sweater up her arm so she could see her watch
without him noticing. Simon liked a bit of pro-
duction with his meetings. Fanfare and other time-
consuming things. Normally, Marie didn't mind

obliging him, but right now, time was money and Simon wasn't paying her enough to chitchat.

"Marie, our viewing audience loves you. People are looking for new gurus of food and style. You make having good taste seem simple and fun, and a little sexy, rather than stuffy or snobby. And of course," he said, grinning, "your looks don't hurt."

What's this? Compliments from Simon? "You feeling all right?" she asked, narrowing her eyes. Simon didn't get warm and fuzzy for no good reason. The guy was a television producer. Behind the khaki pants and plaid shirts from the eighties, he was pretty slick.

"I," he said, spreading his arms out wide, "we," he corrected pointing at her, "are doing just fine."

Marie's bullshit detector went on high alert. *Something is up.*

"What's going on, Simon?"

"Your ratings are way, way up. In fact you've surpassed… " Simon did a little drumroll with his fingers against the edge of his desk and Marie tried not to laugh at him. "Patrick and Ivan."

"Really?" Patrick and Ivan had been ratings horses for almost a year. They were local celebrities. They had dressing rooms.

"When a cooking show beats out two gay interior designers you know you're on to something," he said in all seriousness.

"So you've brought me up here to tell me you're giving me a raise?" she asked and she would be lying if she tried not to sound hopeful. It was all she could do not to sound desperate.

"Sorry," Simon said, cringing. "No raise."

"Then what, Simon? I've got to be back at the restaurant in an hour."

"Well…" He paused and Marie rolled her eyes at his sense of drama. "You are going weekly."

"Weekly?" Marie gasped, suddenly light-headed. She laughed, tried to control it, but couldn't. Who cared about not having a baker? Or the broken dishwasher? She was going to be on television every week!

Simon leaned back in his chair looking gratified and a little smug.

"You said 'no raise.' I'm not doing double the work…"

He put up a hand to stop her. "Same fee per show so it's sort of a raise."

She would take it. She leaned back and felt like she could kiss the water-stained ceiling. She could kiss Simon and his filthy desk. A little more notoriety would bring more people into Marie's Bistro, her bakery/bistro. More customers meant she could pay off her debts, the loan she had to take out last year, maybe even… "A vacation," she breathed.

Since leaving France and the horrible mess she had made there two years ago, Marie had gotten her life under control, had forced herself to grow up, to be an adult. She'd taken on the responsibilities she normally ran from and this was going to be her reward. The bright and shiny beginning of her cooking empire.

"Simon," Marie said, sitting up to look at him, feeling like she was made of fire, "I've got so many ideas, so many things we can do with the show."

"Whoa, before you get carried away, there's a minor change." Simon started digging through the papers on his desk. "Where'd I put that thing?"

His distraction was making Marie nervous. But that could be because she was operating on forty seconds of sleep. "Simon, just tell me what's going on."

"Found it!" He reached to the floor, picked a stack of papers up and turned back around holding one of them out to her. "Look who is on the cover of the *Weekend Magazine.*"

She blinked at the sudden and unwelcome change of subject. Giovanni MacAllister was staring up at her in full eight and a half by eleven glossy from the weekend insert for the *San Francisco Examiner.*

"That's great," she lied, feeling certain she sounded convincing. "Good for him." She attempted to ignore the giant spike of irritation she always felt whenever she thought about him. Van MacAllister owned Sauvignon, a new restaurant across the street from Marie's. And the man had single-handedly made the last six months of her life even more strained and tiring than it had already been.

Calming thoughts, Marie, calming thoughts. She tried a yoga breath, opening up her chest and emptying her belly, but it didn't work. Nothing worked.

Simon was watching her and Marie knew she wasn't fooling him. "You're not still upset about what he said in the *Examiner,* are you?" he asked. "It was one comment and he apologized."

"I'm not upset." Marie shrugged and had to relax her hands from the fists she was making.

"Good, because…"

"I mean, just because he called Marie's Bistro a 'cute little coffee shop' in an international newspaper, why would I be upset?"

Not so good. She had promised herself and her sister, who was tired of hearing about it, that she would not wallow in her anger over Van MacAllister.

Simon winced. "Cute is not so bad…."

"Right." She knew sarcasm was unbecoming, but sometimes it just felt so good. "Cute is fine. Just fine."

"See…"

"If you're a child!" *You're wallowing, Marie,* she thought. *And you're scaring your producer.*

A month ago, a reporter asked Van what he thought of Marie's Bistro and he'd said, "You mean that cute little coffee shop across the street? It's fine if you want a cookie." Marie had been seeing various shades of red since.

"Didn't he apologize?"

"He sent gift certificates for Sauvignon." She shrugged, pretending to be nonchalant, but it was hard considering the apology was almost worse than the original insult. She crossed her legs, arranging her gray jersey skirt over her knees. "Moving on. Why are we even talking about him?"

"Well, we went there last night to see a band…"

"One of his blues bands?" she asked, surprising herself and Simon by nearly yelling.

"I think it was Dixieland jazz," Simon said slowly.

"Whatever it was, you do mean the loud band with horns that played until 1:00 a.m. last night?" She leaned forward in her seat.

"There were horns." He nodded, obviously not sure what he was agreeing to.

"Yeah, horns. 1:00 a.m. I live right across the street from him, Simon, and I have to get up at three to bake bread!" She was beginning to see the music as some sort of torture. "I haven't had a decent three hours sleep in forever. But—" Again she reined herself in, and sat back in the chair. She took a deep breath, imagined waterfalls and waves on the beach and other things that were supposed to relax her but only made her have to go to the bathroom. "He's got the zoning and licensing." She shrugged. "What can you do?"

"I think the bands are all part of his mystique," Simon said and Marie snorted. *Mystique? Please.*

The worst of it wasn't the thing in the paper or

the bands four nights a week. It was that he was in her kitchen. Her dream kitchen, with the old brass hood and the natural lighting. The restaurant space she wanted, had bid on and ultimately lost to Giovanni MacAllister, in an ugly blind bidding war.

So she had bought the place across the street with the smaller kitchen and faulty heating system, and had watched as Van did nothing to the building he'd bought. It had sat empty and vacant while she was sweating in the summer and freezing in the winter across the street, taking out loans and making no money in SoMa—the neighborhood south of Market Street—an untried part of the city.

Six months after she had opened, just as things were beginning to take off for her and the dicey warehouse neighborhood she called home, he had opened Sauvignon to almost instant success. And then he had called Marie's Bistro a "cute little coffee shop" in the paper.

It was a one-two punch that Marie was having a hard time with.

"I can't believe he's on the cover of the *Weekend Magazine*." She hated how she felt about this guy. He shouldn't even register in her life among the blessings and happiness she had, but he did. He was a thorn in her side that she hated admitting to. That he bothered her so much bothered her.

"Marie, you were on the cover three weeks ago.

They called you 'the New Goddess of Good Taste.'"

"Yeah." She smiled, remembering. "That was a good one." She ran her finger over the edge of the magazine, feeling the staple and pressing her thumb against it, trying to squelch all the nasty feelings Van brought out in her. "But it took me a year. A year of freaking out every night."

She didn't talk about the doubt and some of the tears and the bone-deep desire she had almost every day to resort to her old ways and abandon the whole thing. Run off to a beach and sell oranges to tourists.

"Sauvignon has only been open six months." She stopped herself before she started whining that things were unfair. Instead she looked down at Van's arrogant face blown up and glossy.

He wasn't handsome, at least not by her standards, and while the picture of him was flattering, he still wasn't what she would call good-looking. His unsmiling craggy face was...interesting maybe. Perhaps some people could see past those tremendously overgrown eyebrows to the intense eyes beneath them, but she couldn't get past her desire to find the nearest tweezers. His wild black hair with silver shot through it might be attractive. And the scar at his chin was...intriguing. Maybe. But the guy was not handsome.

"He's got great press," Simon said with a wry smile. Marie looked at the headline, having gotten caught up in the out-of-control eyebrows. *Really, someone should have taken the guy in hand years ago.*

"'Van MacAllister,'" she read aloud. "'A man's man. Making haute cuisine rough, ready and masculine.' Oh, give me a break," she moaned. "What does that mean? Masculine haute cuisine?" Marie threw the magazine back on Simon's desk and crossed her arms, dismissing Van MacAllister. "He's grilling meat, Simon. Let's not get carried away."

"Well, some people might say you're just baking bread."

"Simon..."

"I'm not saying it." He pressed his hands to his chest. "You have to admit, though, he's become very popular."

"I don't have to admit anything," she muttered. *He stole my kitchen, made fun of me in the paper and is making it impossible for me to sleep. It's amazing I haven't killed the guy in his sleep. Which is no doubt peaceful and plentiful.*

"You know what they're calling us in the papers, don't you?" she asked, quietly. This was the real rub, the coup de grâce in the bad vibes she felt for Van MacAllister.

Simon had the good grace to look uncomfortable. "Ah..." He cleared his throat and fiddled for a moment with a pen on his desk. "Hip meets homey."

"That's right and guess who's homey?"

He pointed the end of the pen at her.

Marie had written polite but firm letters to the editor until her hand was numb, but the buzz kept building. She was hardly homey, unless one considered the French countryside home. Then, maybe she could be considered homey. But only if it were an outrageously classy, sensual home. That served Thai chicken salad and triple espressos and rhubarb-strawberry bars for dessert. *Okay, maybe that is homey. But it's rhubarb—it is hard to toughen up rhubarb.*

"Why are we even talking about Van MacAllister?"

"Well," he said, steepling his hands against his smiling lips and took a deep breath. "This really is so exciting."

"What is?" Marie didn't even try hiding her confusion and frustration. Simon pointed at the magazine.

"Meet your new cohost."

2

"VERY FUNNY." Marie laughed, a pop of incredulity that came from her gut. She stood to leave. "Are we done? Because I have to get back to the restaurant."

"I'm not joking Marie. The executive producers…"

"Simon, come on," she chastised. But Simon wasn't laughing. In fact, he looked uncomfortable. *Sweaty. He looks sweaty. And very very serious.* Marie sat back down in her chair.

"Oh, no," she breathed. "You're serious."

"I thought you would be excited."

"Excited?" She shook her head at him in disbelief, trying to get her brain around this nonsense. This was worse than getting fired. This was like being overrun by the enemy. Marie felt a strange itch along her skin, an awareness of her heartbeat as it skipped a beat and then doubled. "This is my show, Simon. I built it. It's called *Soul Food with Marie Simmons*, not *Soul Food with Marie Simmons and a Cohost*. And definitely not *Marie Simmons and Van MacAllister*."

"Well, we haven't really worked out the name yet…."

"The name isn't important!" she cried. "You just said it's your most popular segment," she said in a far more reasonable voice. Though it was a bit high-pitched. "I beat out Patrick and Ivan, for crying out loud. Why in the world do you want to mess with a good thing?"

"Marie?" Simon crossed his arms behind his head, looking at her like she was speaking a foreign language. "Six months ago when you signed on you said you would do anything."

"And I did, I did everything you asked. I wore a fruit hat, Simon."

Simon laughed, caught her eye and then coughed uncomfortably. "Right, so why not a cohost?"

"Six months ago I would have wrestled in Jell-O if you wanted me to. But now I have a name and a reputation…." *And a very small, very fragile empire to protect, damn it!* "And you expect me to just hand it over to Van?" It was ludicrous. Outrageous! And she was beginning to hyperventilate.

Six months ago there was no alternative to being laid-back. *Well, there was. It was called homeless,* she thought ruefully. She had nothing to lose then. Marie's Bistro had barely gotten off the ground, she had taken out another loan and was thinking of selling it all and moving to Peru. *Soul Food* was changing all of that. *And now they want to change my show!*

"Marie, your interest is our interest," he told her and Marie almost recoiled in shock at what a used car salesman Simon was turning into right before her eyes. "We just want to...enhance your reputation."

"How?"

"We're looking for male viewers and younger viewers."

"Young?" Marie shook her head, confused for a moment until the lightbulb went on. Simon and the rest of the producers had fallen for the hype. "No, come on Simon..."

"He's the hip in 'hip meets homey.'" Simon shrugged apologetically.

"I'm hip." The adult voice tried to get her under control, but Marie was far too busy beginning a good and honest freak out to listen. "Homey can be hip."

"Only if you're fifty."

Ouch. Marie stood up and began pacing the small area from the bulletin board to the opposite wall. Her blood pressure was climbing through the roof. She put a hand over her heart and felt the hard beat of it against her palm. "Okay, okay I can have a cohost—I can deal with a cohost, but not Van MacAllister. I'll cook with anybody but him." *That's good, Marie. Good compromise. Reasonable.*

"Trust me, Marie."

"Ha!"

"I've got a good feeling about this, Marie. A

good gut feeling." *Like I care about your gut feelings!* she thought, beginning to feel sick.

"It's an awful idea. We won't like each other," she told him, grasping at straws.

"Have you ever really met him?"

"Face to face?" she asked, needlessly. She knew she was creeping toward ridiculous but she had actually made a point never to meet Van MacAllister. Call it pride, call it trying to avoid having a criminal record. Whatever it was, she hadn't actually met him. She could go her whole life hating him from afar.

"My ears are burning," a deep, sarcastic voice said from the doorway behind her.

Simon shot her a look that clearly said "behave," as he stood to shake hands with Van as he entered the room.

"Hello, Giovanni," he said.

"What's he doing here?" Marie asked, realizing suddenly that this had been in the works for a while and she was obviously the last to know. Marie's stomach twisted; she could not have felt more betrayed.

"I invited him to this meeting," Simon answered.

"You've been having secret meetings behind my back?" she cried. Nothing upset her like secret meetings. They were childish and she always ended up getting screwed. "Simon, I can't believe this."

"Just hear us out," Simon urged.

Deep breaths. Calm thoughts. Beaches. Waves. Pup-

pies. Babies. None of it was working. And actually being in the same room with Van was filling her head with very unadult and unreasonable thoughts. Like arson.

Van turned and she got her first real look at him.

Marie was not a woman to get knocked off her feet, though for a moment she was taken aback by the sheer injustice done to him by photographs.

He still wasn't handsome, *not by a long shot*. But he was just standing there and he seemed to take up the entire room. He was dressed in head-to-toe black, which might explain why he seemed so dramatic. He had a whole brooding, smoldering thing that on any other man would have Marie drooling.

Too bad it's wasted on this guy, she thought.

But it was more than the way he looked. Van seemed even sharper than he came off in pictures or from across the street when she spied on him through her windows. Sharp and very focused. It was absurd, but in that moment Van MacAllister, man's man and general all around pig, looked like a pirate.

She hoped, fervently, that Van MacAllister had a small penis. *The man deserves a small penis.*

"Sorry to interrupt," he said with sarcastic politeness. He leaned in toward her and the air when he got close to her crackled, like a nearby storm. The scent of garlic and rosemary lifted off him. She took a deep breath before she could stop herself.

"I gather that you have a problem working with

me?" His eyes were hard and angry, and for a moment she felt like he was seeing right through her. Right into her petty and jealous heart.

"Problem?" She plunked her hands on her hips. "Why in the world would I have a problem with you? Just because you've—"

"Van, we're thrilled you could make it today," Simon said, trying to talk over Marie.

"Speak for yourself, Simon," she said, not taking her eyes off Van, the pirate chef. She was mad, not attracted, and just because she had a hard time looking away from those eyes didn't make her any less angry. In fact, it made it worse. He was a jerk. And he was her type. All of the careful cultivation of Marie's calm and reason vanished.

"Is this about what was printed in *The Examiner?*" he asked. "Because it was taken completely of out context." The look on his face, contrite and apologetic, made his features softer, his dark eyes somehow warmer. But Marie was not going to be fooled.

"Sure it was."

"It was."

"I'm not arguing with you." She crossed her arms, and even shrugged and batted her eyelashes at him.

"Good." He was looking at her carefully and she could feel him picking her apart to see if she were serious.

"Okay!" Simon clapped his hands together and

sat down, but Van remained standing, eyeing her. She eyed him right back. If this was going to be some kind of staring contest, hell if she'd be the first to blink!

The room felt warmer. Simon seemed far away while Van seemed so close she could reach out and touch the zipper of his coat, or the scar on his chin, which was fascinating to look at.

Oh no you don't, not this guy! She tried to wrestle her wayward hormones back in line.

"So, we're ready to get to business?" he asked, like they were going to split a cab or go halves on a pizza. For a moment, Marie had trouble breathing through her anger and disbelief.

"You mean *your* business of taking over part of what I've worked so hard for?"

"Marie!" Simon interjected, but Van held up a hand, curtailing Simon.

"I think we should avoid the words 'taking over,'" Van said calmly.

"Okay, how about this?" she sighed, looking up at the ceiling, pretending to think. "How about the business where I work my ass off for a year and then just when things start to go right for me you get to come along and share. Share? Do we all like that word?" She glanced around, liking the abashed look in Simon's eyes and the muscle that was ticking in Van's jaw.

"Right. So I work hard and you come and share in my success. Which, frankly, I'm thankful for because I was having such a hard time handling it on my own." She took a step closer to him. "If you want to be on TV, Van, go find your own show."

The silence in the office had an echo. She could actually hear the blood beat through her veins, her breath in her lungs.

Van cleared his throat. "Point taken." He nodded, his smile tight.

"Good, then…" She made a move for the door so she could show Van out. "I think our business here is done."

"But—" Van shifted, blocking her way. He crossed his arms over his chest while he pinned her to the wall with his eyes. She felt the sharp popping shocks from the static and animosity surrounding them. "While I certainly appreciate your little speech, let's understand something—I was approached by the producers. By Simon."

"Whom I will never forgive," she threw in with menacing cheer.

"Because your show was missing something." He raised one of those overgrown eyebrows and Marie's fingers twitched. "Something," Van continued, "I can provide."

"Maybe you're right." She resorted back to sarcasm. "Maybe you do have something I need for the show." Marie would bet a new dishwasher on the fact that Van had no idea what he would be doing on TV, because his was not a face for television. "Do you have lots of experience with live TV? Hmmm?"

"No," he said in a low voice.

"No, not lots, or no, not any?" she asked, tilting her head and waiting patiently.

"Simon," Van put his hand on top of a pile of papers on Simon's desk, "you said that she wasn't going to have a problem with this." He jerked his thumb back at Marie. "I call this a problem."

Marie's jaw fell to the floor. Such treason from a man she considered a friend.

"Simon?" she asked, dropping the sarcasm for a moment, and feeling marginally naked in front of Van. "Did you really think that I would be okay with this? That I didn't have any pride in what I had built? In what we had built?"

"I understand that there are—" Simon swallowed audibly "—challenges." He shook his head at Marie like she was a child who had disappointed him. She knew her behavior wasn't exactly sterling, but she had nothing to apologize for. Simon suddenly looked small and wary. "You don't really have a choice."

For the first time since Simon had brought this up, the changes in her show became real. Van was in the room sucking up far too much air and taking up way too much space—imagine what he would do to her show! This was just like France. Men thinking they knew what was best for her. Underestimating her, brushing her aside. Well, she had learned her lesson two years ago and it wasn't going to happen again.

"What happens if I say no?" Marie asked.

"You lose half your airtime, the other half goes to Van."

She could only blink and try to breathe one small mouthful of air at a time. "Wow," she finally said, which was an awful summation of what she was feeling. She looked down at her feet, at the lovely black boots she had paid far too much for. She had to fight the tears that suddenly sprang up. She laughed ruefully. "Just when you start to feel on top of things…"

"Marie…?" There was something different in Van's face, a softness around his hard eyes that wasn't there before.

"Save it, Van. I've got to get back to work at my 'little coffee shop.'" He sucked in a breath and Marie felt the cool victory that comes with saying exactly the right thing at exactly the right time.

The urge to walk out the door, get in her car and drive away from all of this came over her, but that would have been something the old Marie would have done.

"You have twenty-four hours, Marie," Simon cut in, ruining her exit. "Twenty-four hours to make up your mind and do the smart thing. The way the world is making chefs into celebrities you could write your own ticket."

Marie bit her tongue. It was a nice dream. With probably some nice money attached to it. But it wasn't worth it if she had to share it with Van.

"I'll call you, Simon," she said.

She didn't look at Van, so unsure of what she would do or say to him. But as she left, she walked through the smell of him, rosemary and anger, and her body reacted.

She put her right hand over all five of the bracelets on her left wrist, curling her fingers around the silver.

What the hell am I going to do now?

3

MARIE RAN SOME ERRANDS, trying to strike a new deal with the organic dairy guy, but to no avail, and made it back to the restaurant just in time for the late-afternoon rush.

"I need four caps to go," Marie called back to Pete, her mostly silent and dreadlocked part-time employee. As long as Pete didn't have to talk to anybody, he was a fantastic barista. He put together coffee orders almost before they were placed. He nodded at Marie, cranked the steam up on the espresso machine and began steaming milk.

"And a tomato-and-bocconcini salad to go," she told Jodi, her assistant manager, who stood at Marie's elbow putting together salad orders and packaging some of the leftover daily lunch specials.

It all seemed very normal. Susan and Margaret from the accounting office next door were having their late-afternoon coffee break and bitch session. Mr. Malone sat in the far back corner nursing his extra-hot milk chocolate over the newspaper.

Marie was her usual smiley and chatty self, but inside she seethed.

Van MacAllister has a small penis was a constant drumbeat in her head.

"Hello, Mrs. Peters." Marie smiled at the older woman who came in religiously on Tuesdays. Tuesday was clam chowder day and Mrs. Peters, as she frequently told Marie, had been searching for a good clam chowder for years.

Marie was happy to oblige with the best clam chowder in the city, according to *Where* magazine.

"Hello, sweetheart," Mrs. Peters smiled and Marie had to bite her tongue from laughing. The diminutive white-haired woman consistently had orange lipstick all over her teeth. "You were lovely this morning on the television."

"Thanks, Mrs. Peters," Marie said, but waited for the other half of her compliment. The sharp half.

"But you look tired." *And there it is.* "You need to get more rest."

"I couldn't agree with you more."

"You need to find a nice man to help you do all this work."

"Aww…" Marie wrinkled her nose and resisted screaming *Men are ruining my life!* at the eighty-year-old woman. "Men just get in my way."

"Well, if I remember it right, sometimes that's not such a bad thing." Mrs. Peters winked, and Marie hoped she still wanted to have a man get in her way in *that way*, when she was eighty.

No, it isn't a bad thing, Marie thought as she wrapped up the clam chowder and whole-grain rolls. She slipped a few small chocolate-chip cookies in the bag because Marie knew Mrs. Peters liked them and frankly, Marie liked Mrs. Peters.

Men had a purpose that Marie loved. She loved their bodies and their mouths and the things they could do with their hands. She loved monogamous sex in casual relationships, but these days she barely had time to brush her teeth much less find a guy she was attracted to, date a few times, sleep with, and explain why nothing serious would ever come of it.

I like you guys, she would say, *but I just don't trust you. Not with my life or my heart.*

Case in point, Simon and Van. Two men thinking they had her best interests in mind.

She spent the next few hours replaying the scene in Simon's office, but editing in wittier and sharper things to say to Van. The game was ultimately frustrating, but so very satisfying right now.

"Hey, Marie," Marie shook off the scene in her head where she punched Van in the nose and turned to Pete. "You ah…mind if I take off now?" he asked. He glanced down at his watch. "I've been here since six."

"Oh my God, Pete." She looked at her own watch. It was quarter past six in the evening. Twelve hours. "Go, go. I can't believe you stayed so long."

"Yeah, well, we're busy." He shrugged, his green Rage Against the Machine T-shirt wrinkled on his thin shoulders. "See you on Thursday."

"Good night, Pete. Thanks so much." Pete grabbed his beat-up backpack from the cabinet under the cash register and shuffled out the door.

Marie followed him and flipped the sign on the door from Open to Closed. She fought the strong urge she had to fall down on the floor for a little nap. Just a short one, right there on the floor until Van's blues bands woke her up.

"All right, Marie!" Jodi came into the dining room from the kitchen carrying the large rolls of plastic wrap and pushing the full mop bucket across the hardwood floors with her foot. "Let's clean up and get out of here. I got a date."

"Oh?" Marie pushed away from the door, feeling a happy lift in her low mood. Her sex life, once something of a legend, had been reduced to the stories Jodi told her while they mopped the floor.

Sad, Marie, that's just sad.

"Somebody new?" Marie asked, reaching to help Jodi carry the plastic wrap.

"No." Jodi pushed her funky black glasses up higher on her nose. "I've known him for a while, but this is our first *date* date." Jodi shrugged, trying to play it cool but she looked far too happy. Actually she was glowing. Marie recognized the glow of the young and foolish.

Be careful, she wanted to say. *Please be careful with your heart, Jodi.* She was young, about the age Marie was when she met Ian in France. About the age Marie last felt that kind of glow.

"Oh," Marie teased, "a *date* date."

"You remember those?" Jodi asked over her shoulder, obviously taking shots at Marie's nonexistent dating life.

"You're hilarious. Get mopping."

"I don't understand, Marie." Jodi started putting the wrought-iron chairs up on tiled café tables and as she lifted the chairs her shirt rode up her body revealing the pretty flowered vine tattoo she had curling around her back. And the dim lighting made her pink hair glow.

How can people say I'm not hip? Marie thought. *Look at my staff.*

"Every guy in here falls in love with you," Jodi continued.

"Who?" Marie asked.

"Those two hot cops that come in for lunch on Thursdays. Why don't you go on a date with one of them?"

"Because they're gay."

"No. Really?" Jodi asked, a little crestfallen.

"Words to live by Jodi—when it seems too good to be true, it usually is."

"But what about…?"

"I'm too tired to date." Marie closed the subject and yawned so big her jaw nearly cracked. It was mostly the truth. The rest of it had to do with Ian and she didn't want to think about it.

Marie reached under the cash register and turned up the stereo both to stop Jodi from asking more questions and to stop herself from dwelling on the past.

Soon Jodi was singing along with the old Annie Lennox songs and Marie started covering her salads, deciding what would have to be made fresh in the morning and which had another day left in them. While she covered up her green-apple-and-poppy-seed coleslaw, Marie had one of those moments she had been having more and more frequently.

She looked around at her dimly lit place, decorated with all of her favorite light colors, at the shelves filled with bottles of her salad dressings and chutneys; the antique espresso maker that cost her a small fortune but lent a one-of-a-kind air to the small room, and the tiled tabletops with the mismatched wrought-iron chairs. All of it was hers. And part of her, a little tiny part with a loud voice, wished it weren't.

We've talked about this, Marie, her adult voice piped up. *You want to end up like your mother?* The answer to that of course was a resounding *no!*

Her mother, Belinda, moved Marie and Marie's older sister, Anna, every few months when they were kids, leaving behind bad jobs and worse men only to find new ones in different towns. It was a trend Marie had started following until she found herself heartbroken and penniless in France.

She had run from that broken heart right into the restaurant business.

She was a good boss and a good chef. But, to own so much, to be responsible for so much was new for her. For twenty-seven years she wasn't responsible for anything. Not a pet, not a plant, not her love life, not her career. And when she took this on a year ago, she really had no idea what she was in for. She kept telling herself it would get better, she was sure it would. She would hire another baker. More staff. And the pressure would be off. But then the dishwasher broke and Ariel ran off with the cash.

And, of course there was Van.

The CD was on shuffle and Annie Lennox faded away, replaced by the quieter Ella Fitzgerald.

"So you really don't think you're going to do the show anymore?" Jodi asked, dumping the dustpan out in the trash.

Marie sighed. Do the show, don't do the show. She was going crazy thinking about it. She wanted to, of course she did. A weekly show. It was a dream come true. But Van MacAllister was really much more of a nightmare.

"I don't know," she said honestly. She flicked the lights off in the salad case and part of the room went a little darker.

"That guy's got a lot of nerve, huh?" Jodi asked. She wrenched the handle on the mop bucket, squeezing out water, and she started to mop the hardwood floors. "Talk about piggybacking someone's success."

"You're telling me," Marie murmured.

"But you can take him," Jodi said.

"Of course I can take him." There was never any question in Marie's mind that she could take Van MacAllister, the glorified barbecue chef.

"So do the show, but make sure it's on your terms." Jodi stopped mopping for a second, blowing her pink bangs off her forehead. "'Cause it would be a great show, the two of you. The potential for loads of chemistry and that's what it's all about, isn't it?" Jodi shrugged and turned to wheel the mop bucket back to the kitchen. "Get it all in writing, Marie," Jodi yelled. Marie heard the water being thrown out the back door into her herb garden while Jodi's words resonated in her head.

Get it all in writing. Of course. It was so adult, no wonder she didn't think of it.

"'Cause a weekly half-hour show is still a weekly half-hour show," Jodi came back into the dining room, wiping her hands on her low-slung blue jeans. "Right?"

"How'd you get so smart, Jodi?" Marie asked, feeling very fond of her punk assistant manager.

"Don't let the pink hair fool you," Jodi smiled, her hands on her thin hips. "Top third of my class at Berkeley." She exhaled and shrugged. "I'm off. See you in the morning."

Jodi grabbed her bag and scooted for the door. Marie started counting the totals for the night, wondering if she could actually do the show, handle Van and build her empire at the same time. She was good, but was she that good?

The bell rang over the door as Jodi opened it. "'Night Jodi," Marie called out as she counted change.

"Good ni…" Jodi trailed off and Marie glanced up. "There's someone here for you." Jodi stepped back into the restaurant and Van MacAllister followed her in the door.

It was like having the Antichrist walk in the room.

"We're closed," she said.

He had changed from his all-black civilian clothes to an all-black chef jacket and pants. His name and Sauvignon were embroidered in red over his heart.

"I noticed, but I was hoping we could talk." He took a few more steps toward her and the currents shifted. The air was heavier. It seemed like the entire atmosphere was pressing against her.

"I haven't decided about the show," she told him, hoping to get rid of him and his strange energy.

He nodded, but didn't say anything. Instead, he was looking around the room, his eyes cataloging everything, measuring their worth in a way that had Marie wanting to run around throwing herself in front of her chutneys.

It was amazing how the inherent femininity of the place made Van seem that much more masculine. Tall, rangy, not quite handsome. Commanding in a mysterious sort of way, he

was only more so in the pale blue room surrounded by the very real-looking fake grapevine
she had wrapped around the rustic wooden pil-
lars and ceiling beams. He reached up and
tugged on the grapevine and a piece fell off in
his hand.

"Sorry," he said, wincing, slipping the fake vine
into his pocket.

Deep inside Marie's head things began short-
circuiting.

"So Van, we don't have anything to talk about."
She grew even more annoyed when his silence
continued. He bent to examine the labels on her
homemade vinaigrette.

"Are people really buying this stuff?" he asked,
like he was peering into the underwear rack at a
used clothing store.

"Yes, they do."

"Amazing." His tone implied he couldn't believe it.

Marie tried deep yoga breaths, combined with
calming thoughts and it did nothing to combat her
irritation. "So feel free to show yourself out." Jodi
was beginning to laugh and Marie shrugged at her
assistant. What was she supposed to do? "Van…"

"Your place is beautiful, Marie. Absolutely
beautiful. I've seen pictures, but they don't do it
justice."

Marie's mouth fell open. She was so startled
that she couldn't say anything for a few moments.

Finally, when she was getting her breath back to respond, he turned to her.

"I came to apologize for my part in the ambush today." With a sheepish smile he held out a bottle of wine. She shifted her weight to one leg and leaned against the long wooden counter, feeling like the ground had moved under her feet. *Van, apologizing? Bearing gifts? Maybe I was wrong....*

She turned to Jodi, who was staring at Van like the man had come in on a golden carriage. "Jodi, go ahead and go home," she murmured.

"You going to be okay?" Jodi asked under her breath as they watched Van turn and bend down in front of the dessert case and Marie took a moment to admire the view. Awful eyebrows, but not too bad from the back.

"Why wouldn't I?" she asked.

Van straightened and looked up at Marie's ceiling. "He looks...dangerous," Jodi breathed.

Marie frankly couldn't agree more but she rolled her eyes and pushed her assistant toward the door. "You need some sleep. See you tomorrow."

"Don't do anything I wouldn't do," Jodi whispered and ran out the door.

He walked over to the dark salad case. "I can leave—after we talk." He tapped the glass with his finger. "You buy this used? Looks used. Can you turn the light on?"

Unbelievable. The guy was just...unbelievable. Marie straightened and strolled over to the salad case, she rested her arms on it and her head was close to his.

"I'm going to give you the benefit of the doubt," she said with a smile that was pretty hard to muster up, "and guess that you have no idea how rude you are being."

He stood upright, obviously alarmed. "I'm sorry," he said, wincing. "I am. I am sorry. Marie, I did not mean to come in here and alienate you further. I've never been here before. It's…" He took a deep breath, his hand touched his mouth and then the scar at his lip.

That's adorable, she thought, knowing that she shouldn't fall for this little show of regret. "Truce. Honestly." He put the wine bottle on top of the case and she noted that he had brought some serious ammunition with a hundred-dollar bottle of Shiraz.

"Let me pour you some wine. I can have some of your marinated root salad everyone in the city is raving about and we can talk about *AMSF*?"

He smiled, sincerely with warmth and it changed everything. His face became something much more than interesting. He became arrestingly handsome.

"Marie?" She realized she had been staring at Van for a few silent moments.

"Sure," she said with far too much volume, suddenly in overdrive, despite her better sense that told her that sharing a bottle of wine with this guy in her current tired and marginally attracted state would only come to no good. "Why not?"

"Is that a mural?" he asked pointing up at the painting on her ceiling.

"Yes."

"Are those…?" He tilted his head and squinted.

"Yes, they are cherubs wearing aprons," she told him on a huffy breath. She almost wished he would go back to rude; she could handle rude Van.

"So?" Van looked around at all the chairs up on the tables and then at her. He raised one of those eyebrows in a silent command/query.

"Go ahead," she said, gesturing to the chairs. "I'll grab some glasses."

"No root salad?" he asked and she couldn't quite make out the tone in his voice. Laughter?

"No root salad," she told him. She grabbed two of her red wineglasses and came back to the table. Van had taken down both chairs and from one of the big front pockets of his black chef's jacket he pulled out a corkscrew. With smooth, deft effort that Marie was somehow compelled to watch, he had the bottle open in moments.

"The photos of you don't quite do you justice," he said, seemingly focused on the task at hand. Marie's eyes narrowed. She should have guessed that Van would be smarmy. Genetics had been kind to her for some reason and most men seemed to believe that the size of her breasts had an inverse relationship to the size of her brain. She waited for some wildly inappropriate comment about her boobs or her eyes or…

"You're much taller than in the photos."

She swallowed, her anger lessening as his gaze rested a little too long and a little too warm on her face. There were things he wasn't saying.

"You look shorter," she said.

"Let's allow that to breathe." Van set the bottle down on the edge of the table with a casual ownership that put her teeth on edge. He crossed his legs with a comfortable masculine grace.

Short and sweet, Marie.

"We don't have that kind of time, Van." She grabbed the bottle and poured, expertly, exactly four ounces of wine in each glass.

"Salute." She tapped her glass to his and then sipped the dark red liquid. It was fantastic, mellow, dark and oaky. The kind of wine she loved. "It's wonderful."

"It would be even better in ten minutes," he snapped, the sharpness of the comment belied by the tone of his voice, like he knew what she was doing. He smiled wickedly at her over the edge of his wineglass, his long fingers holding the delicate stem as he swirled the wine.

Oh my, she thought before she could stop herself.

"Let's cut to the chase here, Van." Marie sat back in her chair. She'd drink a glass of wonderful wine and send the pirate chef on his way. She opened her mouth to let him have it.

"You're a coward," Van interjected into the silence. It seemed he was bent on cutting to a different chase.

4

"Excuse me?" There was no way he just called her, a woman who had climbed mountains and rafted rivers and started her own business all before the age of thirty, a coward.

"You heard me." He took another sip of wine and set his glass back on the table "You're scared that you can't take the comparisons...."

"Comparisons?" Marie repeated because her ears were still ringing with the word *coward. Is this a challenge? Is he challenging me?* Marie's inner DeNiro started to get antsy.

"Sure. It's been coming up more and more in the papers, that my place is—" he shrugged as if he couldn't help himself "—stylish, and Marie's Bistro is..." He wrinkled his nose just a bit. "Quaint."

"There is nothing wrong with quaint," Marie told him, trying not to sound righteous. "Perhaps you missed the headlines calling me the new goddess of good taste?"

"No, but I saw the one that called you fussy."

"Look! You jerk." Marie's wineglass hit the table with a ping. *So much for adult.* "This is precisely why I am not doing the show. I will not spend any more time in the company of a man I don't like…"

"Not even if it means paying off your loans? Moving out of the apartment over your restaurant?" Again with the eyebrow, again with the slight rise in her core temperature. "Marie, you had to turn an old warehouse into this…" He looked around and Marie gritted her teeth. "Charming space. I know, I did the same thing and it wasn't cheap."

"Your place hardly needed any work," she said and then bit her tongue. He didn't know who he had been haggling with in that bidding war and he didn't need to know.

"That's what I thought until I bought the place, which was almost completely renovated, and then the sewage drains collapsed."

Marie laughed and then clapped a hand over her mouth. Van's look indicated that he didn't think the sewage situation was all that funny. She quickly tried to compose her face into something convincingly sympathetic, but inside she was howling.

"It took three months to fix and another two to get rid of the smell. It cost me thousands."

Marie took a sip of wine to hide her grin. Suddenly a broken dishwasher didn't seem so bad.

"That is—" she worked hard at not laughing "—awful."

"Right, so this show and the revenue could come in pretty handy."

"*AMSF* isn't going to pay that much money," Marie pointed out.

"But, Marie," Van said, leaning forward, his black eyes focused on her in a way that made Marie's heart beat a little faster, "you and I both know it's not about the salary from the show. It's about what the show could do for us. Imagine if it takes off. Imagine Marie's Bistro crowded every day for brunch, not just Sundays. Imagine people lined up three deep around your bakery counter, not just at 3:00 p.m. but all day long. Imagine tourists coming to Marie's Bistro, because the whole nation had taken notice."

It was like he had opened her head and saw her dreams. Her cooking empire. She was imagining lines out the doors, expanding her catering business, hiring an accountant. She imagined sleeping for three days. On a beach. In Mexico.

"Imagine being debt-free." Van leaned back. "Free and clear." He shook his head, a little wrapped up in the daydream himself.

"How bad is your debt?" Marie asked.

"Bad enough that…ah…" He took a sip of wine, flicked a dried tomato seed off his pants. Marie perked up. "I…ah…am asking you to do the show. You are getting to be a big star." Marie

could only blink as he continued. "And I understand that I am riding your coattails here, but I
think with the weekly exposure you and I could
take off."

She took her time, sipping her wine, fiddling
with one of her silver bracelets, grappling with
what he had just said to her. He had laid himself
bare, vulnerable, and she couldn't ruin the moment by saying "gotcha."

A woman isn't handed a plum like this everyday.

Jodi's words from earlier, about getting it all in
writing came back to her. *This just might work,* she
thought staring at the magnified tiles through the
bottom of her wineglass. *It just might.*

Finally she glanced up at him and almost
laughed out loud. Clearly the man's pride did not
sit well in his stomach. He looked like a food-poi-
soning victim.

He swallowed, looked up at her cherubs and
took a deep breath. "Please?" he asked in a stran-
gled voice.

Marie laughed great big belly laughs like she
hadn't in weeks. "Oh, that was hard, wasn't it?"
She wiped a tear from the corner of her eye.

"Are you going to do it or not?" he nearly
barked.

"Come now, Van. Surely you've heard the one
about honey versus vinegar?" One corner of her
mouth lifted and she took a sip of wine.

"What do you want?"

Aha, now we're getting somewhere.

"No more blues on Wednesday and Thursday nights." She reached over and poured more wine into their glasses.

"Don't be ridiculous," he scoffed.

"You're the one who just said please."

"I'll shut it down at one."

"Ten."

"Midnight."

"Ten."

"Fine, ten. On Wednesday. You can't have Thursday."

Which was exactly what she was going for. She grinned at him. "That wasn't so hard was it?"

"So, that's it, you'll do it?" he asked, his eyes narrowed.

"Not so simple, Van." She shook her head at him and stood up. She found a notebook and a pen by the cash register and brought them back to the table where Van was looking at her warily.

"I learned something important today," she told him as she flipped through her notebook and found an empty page. "Simon, despite saying he has my best interests at heart, is only looking after himself and ratings. Which—" she shrugged "—I can't blame him for. So, I've got to take care of myself."

"Should I have my lawyer here?"

"Don't worry, I'll have my lawyer draw something up," she said and meant it. No more Mr. Nice Guy.

"Marie?" She looked up, arrested for the moment by the sudden wild, vibrant energy that was pouring out of him. He was lit up and Marie felt her body reacting. Her heartbeat sped up and her skin flushed with blood. "Are you going to do the show?"

"With a few minor stipulations." She nodded. "Yes. I am."

"Well then, a toast…" He held up his wineglass.

"Let's hold off on the celebrating." Marie pushed his glass back down. "First things first, there will be no secret meetings. You and I will be present every time one or the other meets with Simon."

Van cocked his head to the side and studied her. "You're not very trusting, are you?" he asked.

"Oh, on the contrary, I'm probably trusting to a fault."

He laughed. "Could have fooled…"

"Just not with men and business." Again Marie felt the strange physical nature of his gaze, like he was touching her, lifting her hair, looking in her pockets to see what she was hiding.

"I'm trustworthy, Marie," he told her seriously and Marie swallowed hard. It was her nature to believe him. It was her nature to believe everyone. But it simply didn't pay to trust everyone.

She shrugged. "We'll see." She returned to her pad of paper and her lists of demands she believed would truly protect her from Van MacAllister.

THE RESTAURANT WAS CLOSED on Mondays and Marie, after going in to feed her sourdough starter and proof some of the other dough, refused to stay and work on the books. So she had called her sister, Anna, and now they were shopping. Usually Marie loved to shop. But not today.

It was her first day off in what seemed like months and the last thing she wanted to do was spend it looking at crib liners. But she hadn't spent any quality time with her sister in what seemed like forever, and all Anna wanted to do was shop for the baby and eat. So that's what they did.

"I like this one." Anna was looking at a baby's room all done up in a western theme. It was a cowboy massacre—ten-gallon hats, lassos and disembodied horse heads were strewn everywhere. "It's cute, right?" Anna blinked her big blue eyes at Marie. *You poor thing,* Marie thought, *you just don't have a clue.*

"It's fine if you're raising Clint Eastwood."

"No good?" Anna looked back at the crib and idly rubbed her pregnant belly. "I kind of like it."

"Well," Marie sighed and linked arms with her sister, propelling her down the isle. "That's why you brought me. To save you from your own bad taste."

"You're right," she agreed with one final look over her shoulder. "I swear it's like something has taken over my head these days. I thought they were kidding when they talked about pregnancy brain."

"Sweetheart, you've always had bad taste," Marie joked, laughing when Anna scowled.

Marie looked over the heads of the crowd of women surrounding them at Baby and Bough, a fashionable one-stop shopping experience for the expectant mother. Or as Marie was beginning to think of it: Hell on Earth.

"Let's get out of here," Anna said on a sigh. "I want beef." Marie rolled her eyes. Anna, thin as a rail except for the giant belly she was now sporting, had the metabolism of a groundhog. If she didn't eat every ten minutes her body would start eating itself. And now, pregnant and just filled with cravings, her appetite had become a not-so-funny joke between Marie and Anna's husband Sam.

"It's ten o'clock on a Monday."

"I know," Anna said, looking down at her watch, "I should really be at work."

"No!" Marie insisted. "No work, we promised each other." They emptied out of the store onto busy Church Street.

If she let Anna dictate the course of events, they'd be eating all day and if Marie had to look at food or step into another restaurant, she'd lose it. Marie made an executive decision.

"We'll get you a sandwich. I've got an idea." Marie put up her hand to hail a cab, not giving Anna any chance to dig in her heels.

"I don't like the sound of that," Anna said hesitantly.

"Trust me."

Anna snorted. "I really don't like the sound of that."

Thirty minutes later they were easing their feet into the whirlpool baths that were the delicious precursor to a deluxe pedicure at Indulgence Spa. Or as Marie was thinking of it: Heaven on Earth.

"This is ridiculous. I can't even see my toes," Anna groused, but sighed happily as she put her feet into the hot bubbly water.

"Sam can."

"True," she finally agreed and leaned back in her massage chair. "If I fall asleep here, don't wake me up."

Marie smiled and closed her eyes. This was relaxing. Instantly gratifying relaxation with bright red toes at the end of it. Pedicures were a gift, a blessing. The air smelled like herbs, a woman was soon going to come around and rub her feet and she was with her sister. What could be better?

Nude men, Marie answered her own question. *Good-looking ones with reasonably trim eyebrows who don't talk.*

Anna groaned and shifted in the chair before her eyes shut. Her hands fell off the hand rest and dangled.

"I'm glad to see you embracing the pedicure," Marie said, laughing at her sister. Any moment Anna was going to be asleep or drooling. Or both.

"It's the chair," she sighed. "I feel strong things for this chair."

Marie reached across the small space between their massage chairs and squeezed Anna's hand. Anna hummed and squeezed back.

"What's going on with the show?" Anna asked.

"We have a meeting with Simon tomorrow."

"Any idea what you'll be doing?"

"None, but I am hoping it's like *Soul Food*, you know?" She tried to encapsulate all that the show was to her with an airy wave of her hand. "Something different. Who wants to see us in chef jackets cooking chicken?"

"I'd like to see Van out of his chef jacket," Anna said lecherously.

Marie sat up. "You've never met the guy."

"Sure I did. Sam and I went to dinner at Sauvignon a few nights ago. He's quite something." Anna laughed and lazily opened her eyes.

"Sauvignon?" Marie gasped, turning on her sister with real horror. "You went to Sauvignon?" *Was there no loyalty in this family, no shame?*

"Yeah, we wanted steak. I thought you forgave him for what he said in the paper."

Marie shut her eyes and turned up the massage pressure in her chair. "I have. I am, in fact, glad you went."

"You have to admit, Marie," Anna said. "The man is gorgeous."

"I don't know if I would say gorgeous." Marie contemplated her mental image of the man, only really willing to budge so far on her opinion of him, no matter what her hormones were saying. "Striking perhaps."

"So you've noticed."

"It's hard not to notice the guy's looks. His eyebrows could house a family of birds."

"I think he's sexy," Anna murmured. "Very, very sexy."

Marie thought about him in the dim lighting of her restaurant, his eyes alive and warm on her face. She was getting heated just thinking about it.

"I won't argue with sexy."

"So, you going to…?" Anna trailed off and Marie opened one eye to see what she was implying. Anna was leering, like a teenage boy, which meant sex.

"No, I am not going to." Marie shut her eye. "I am being an adult, Anna." She barely got the words out before Anna was howling.

"I'm sorry, I just think it's hilarious when you say you're going to be an adult. It's like when you say you're going to be reasonable."

"I don't think there is anything funny about this. I am not going to jeopardize my cooking empire for a one-night stand with Van MacAllister."

"You don't know it's going to be a one-night stand."

"Anna," Marie grabbed her sister's hand and made her look at her. "Anybody would be a one-night stand at this point. I don't have the time or the inclination for involvement." She said the word like it was dirty, which, having been badly burned by Ian and France, and far too busy to contemplate getting back up on the relationship bicycle, it was.

"That's too bad, Marie," Anna said, her voice becoming serious. "Because involvement is really, really good."

Marie groaned and closed her eyes. "Stop," she moaned. "I can't take any more stories of wedded bliss."

"I am just saying…"

"Let's talk about your little cowboy," Marie said, changing the subject. Talking about the baby could keep Anna occupied for hours.

"That bedroom was a little much, wasn't it?" Anna agreed.

"I'll say, pilgrim." She gave her John Wayne impression a shot and Anna cringed. Marie watched her sister absently run her hands across her belly and wiggle her toes in the water. Two years ago Anna had been a wound-up and locked-down workaholic with no life and very little joy.

"You look happy," Marie whispered feeling a sort of melancholy that took her by surprise. She was happy. In a different way. Maybe not in the glowing-with-love-and-life-and-child way. But there were other ways to feel fulfilled and satisfied.

"I am," Anna answered with a small smile that spoke a language Marie didn't understand.

Marie closed her eyes and tried to concentrate on the pedicure. *Weekly show, thriving business. What more do I need?*

5

GIOVANNI MACALLISTER LEANED against the door of his black, mint-condition 1963 MG TD convertible. It was his pride and joy and his father's pride and joy before him. He gulped back his substandard espresso (his mother would shoot him dead if she knew he went into a chain coffee shop for espresso) and wished with every fiber of his tired being for a cigarette.

Just one. A half of one. A drag. At the moment he would be happy with some secondhand smoke. A picture of a cigarette.

It was times like these that he truly had no idea why he'd quit. What were a few more years of this agony worth at the end of his life?

Van weighed the blessings of extra years at age eighty, when he was senile and wearing diapers, or the extreme pleasure nicotine and tar would give him right now. He started patting down his black leather jacket searching for his emergency smoke, then he remembered he smoked it after his little negotiation session with Marie at her restaurant a week ago.

He just did not know what to make of her. She was obviously pissed at him, and part of him didn't blame her for putting the screws to him, but holy cow, he'd apologized a million times for what was in the paper and he'd said please. What more could she want? Well, blood obviously from the way she'd had him sign those demands the other night. His mind ran over her list of "stipulations" and he could feel his temperature rise.

He agreed to every one of those demands. Ridiculous ones that really made him question her sanity, like the clause that said if anyone had to wear a fruit hat it would be him.

He was protective over what he did but she took things a step further. He couldn't make public appearances without her, he couldn't meet with Simon without her. He could discuss the show but not her with the press.

That woman was wound up tight about trusting him. He got the impression that she didn't particularly trust men in general.

Which was fine. He didn't trust her, either. Apart from being beautiful, truly one of the most stunning women he had ever seen, she was the kind of chef (and he did use the word lightly) he hated.

The whole world had become tinkerers. People no longer took the time or energy required to really learn something, or know something. Someone told Marie Simmons that she was a good cook and she got some loans and made a business out of it. Now he was not saying that she did not have taste, she obviously did.

His place could use some of her charm. As it was, he kept the lights dim and the food impeccable so people wouldn't see that the red walls were actually sort of pink. He was color-blind and on a budget—what could he do?

But what Marie Simmons wasn't, was a chef. A chef was someone like Mitch Palyard, Van's mentor and the grandfather of West Coast cuisine. He was a visionary and an artist, and would no doubt be appalled that Van was signing on to work with Betty Crocker. Van smiled in anticipation of that discussion with the old man.

But first he had to get through this meeting with Simon and Marie without strangling her with her gorgeous hair. But between her taste and his cooking, they would probably be able to put together a classy show that would help him with his mountain of debt.

And if he became a household name in the bargain, he wasn't about to complain.

"Hello, Giovanni." She was right in front of him. He blinked at her, stunned by her beauty. Cream. Her skin looked like fresh, cool cream. For a moment the urge to touch her, to run the palm of his hand down the flushed warm skin of her throat, was more powerful than his urge for a cigarette.

"You always wear black?" she asked, looking him up and down in his black pants and black T-shirt.

He shrugged. "You always dress like a gypsy?" he asked.

"Yes, I do," she said with a short laugh. He realized last week that she had been subdued with her long gray skirt, and the gorgeous purple sweater that made her eyes look like gems.

The silver bracelets were obviously a uniform of sorts; he had never seen her, or a picture of her, without them. Today she wore a loose white linen shirt, open at the throat so the huge turquoise necklace she was wearing took center stage. Her hair was tied back with an orange ribbon and her dark denim skirt was short. Blessedly short.

She looked exotic. *She looks erotic*, he corrected himself. She looked like sex. She was the kind of woman men paint and write operas about. She was Carmen. She was Rosalyn. Her body alone was worthy of an opera. She was tall and curvy but she carried herself like a queen. A gypsy queen. There was nothing sexier to Van than a confident woman.

"Do you smoke?" he asked, overwhelmed again by a craving.

"No."

He sighed. There was no one left in California with a tobacco addiction.

"I'm glad to see that you're not holding a grudge about the other night."

"Marie," he said, pushing himself off the bumper of his car and standing closer to her, appreciating the way she smelled and the way her blue eyes got wider the nearer he was. "My name is Giovanni MacAllister. I am Scottish and Italian. Holding grudges is what I do." He gave himself a very pleasant moment of watching her gape like a fish. Finally, the woman was speechless.

"Shall we go?" He gestured toward the building—and their combined futures—with his arm.

TWENTY MINUTES LATER, as they sat in Simon's cluttered office, Van felt the rug get pulled out from under him.

"Absolutely not." Van shook his head.

"I love it," Marie said at the same time. "I'm in."

Van shot a horrified look at her. "You're in?" He couldn't believe it. "You're supposed to be the goddess of good taste."

She shrugged. "I think it will be fun. And, I think it can be tasteful."

"The Crocodile Hunter meets Bobby Flay is not tasteful." Van threw Simon's pitch back at him.

"I think it sounds great," Marie laughed and even clapped her hands in front of her. "I'm totally thrilled."

She said "totally." He was going to work with a crazy gypsy woman who was *not* a chef and said "totally." This was not part of his vision. No, this was the exact opposite of his vision.

He thought this would be a little cooking show, a few reviews of new restaurants. Telling housewives new quick ideas for chicken. He would talk about good food made simple and Marie would talk about…whatever Marie wanted to talk about. Salad or something.

"I don't understand what the problem is," Marie said, looking between Van and Simon.

"Obviously," he scoffed, but she kept talking.

"It's you and me eating cobra hearts in Chinatown and going out with the fishing boats to get the freshest fish and looking for the best tongue sandwich in the city. It's adventure and food and San Francisco. It sounds perfect." She stared right at him with her wide blue eyes and her short skirt and he had to try to control his breathing. She looked so young. And gorgeous. Was she trying to provoke him?

"No one wants to see us eat cobra heart or tongue sandwiches. I don't want to eat cobra heart or tongue sandwiches," he said through his teeth.

"Those were just two ideas…." Simon interjected.

"Well—" she cocked her head at Van "—who is the coward now, huh?"

"I am not a coward, Marie. What I am is a chef and a businessman and *as* a chef and a businessman I am saying that the Crocodile Hunter does not serve my purpose. I run a classy restaurant that appeals to a person of a certain taste."

"Shut up, you do not. You're a barbecue chef."

Van for a moment could only see red. His blood leaped nearly right out of his veins. She had a lot of nerve…. He leaned across the arm of the chair toward her. "What did you…?"

She leaned right back at him until there was barely a space between them. "Perhaps if you were—"

"Stop it," Simon shouted and both Van and Marie turned to look at him. "Here's what we're going to do. You are going to separately put together a list of shows that you would like to do. The only requirement being that they are about food and San Francisco and only two of your choices actually show you guys cooking. We're trying to make things different here, guys, we don't want to do the same old thing."

"Sounds good." Marie nodded her head and started digging around her giant green-and-yellow patchwork bag.

"Then what?" Van asked, dreading what Marie might think up.

"Then, we will discuss matters rationally." Simon's eyes darted meaningfully at both of them. "We've got ten half-hour shows. We're hoping to do some live but obviously some will have to be pretaped. So come up with what you like and then we will compromise."

Marie looked at Van, batting her long eyelashes. "Compromise? You do know what that word means, don't you?"

"Simon, you better control—"

"Listen to me." Simon took a few deep breaths. "I thought this would work because there is a serious chemistry between you two, but if you continue to behave this way, it's off. I don't need two childish prima donnas going to work on my ulcers. I just don't need it." Van's mouth dropped open. Who knew the little plaid producer had such a bite?

"Sorry, Simon," Marie muttered.

"Yeah, sorry Simon," Van seconded.

"Here." Simon dug around his messy desk, knocking pencils to the ground, and finally found two notebooks that he handed to them. "Make a list."

Minutes slowly ticked down as Van wrote out every idea he'd had over the last few days. He saw Marie writing furiously and he fought the urge to peek over her shoulder to see what she was putting down.

"All right, Van, what have you got?" Simon asked after a few minutes.

"Well," he said, sending an arch look Marie's way. She only rolled her eyes at him and made another note in her notebook. "First, I have what I think is a good solid beginning—Surprising Chicken Recipes. We can do interesting—"

Marie laughed and slapped her notebook against her knee. Van's temper started to simmer. "What is so funny?"

"Chicken hasn't been surprising since the Middle Ages." She shook her head. "Veto."

Van looked at Simon for support but Simon was nodding in agreement with Marie. "Not quite what we're looking for. Though—" he paused and raised a finger "—how about Tastes Like Chicken? Different meat from turkey to alligator or snake or…" He waved his hand, obviously at a loss. "Whatever else might taste like chicken."

Marie nodded in emphatic agreement. "I think it sounds fun."

"It's not a bad idea," Van said, which seemed to be translated in Simon's head as a resounding yes.

"Great." Simon looked pleased and made a note on his notebook. Van suddenly felt like one of the lemmings in the middle of the pack who didn't think cliff-diving was such a good idea. "What else have you got?"

Van looked back down at his list. He was ready to fight for the next one; it was an important health consideration today. "Okay, how about Making Your Garden Organic. We can do things on container gardens and what organic really means and visit some of the organic farmers in the area."

"I've got that one, too," Marie said and Van's gaze flew to hers.

"Really?" He wasn't sure if he was more shocked that they agreed on something or that organic was a consideration of hers.

"Of course," she said, but her tone said *of course, jerkface.* "Maybe we can have a blind taste test with organic versus nonorganic." She shrugged.

"It's not really sexy but it might work." Simon added it to his list. "Marie, what else have you got?"

"Extreme Eating to Go."

"Veto," Van said immediately.

"Why?"

"I am going to veto anything with the word *extreme* in the title. This is a cooking show not—"

"Fine," she agreed through her teeth. She scratched two more things off her list. Van lifted his gaze to the water-stained ceiling. *What the hell have I done?*

FIVE HOURS, THREE COFFEES and a half a turkey sandwich later, Marie stormed out of the offices into the parking lot. Van was hot on her heels.

"You are being unreasonable," she told him, battling her frustration. She threw her bag over her shoulder and lifted her hair out of the way of the strap.

"Well, if you want to call smart and business-minded *unreasonable* then fine," he called out after her.

"Yeah, well you—" She stopped. He was no longer right behind her and it was ridiculous that she knew, but she did. Because she couldn't feel him there. The man had the strangest effect on her body; it was like static electricity, sharp and constant.

She turned and found him harassing a young techie-looking guy who was having a smoke at a smaller side entrance to the building.

"Look, man, I'll give you a smoke," the guy was saying. He dug through his pockets, grabbing his pack. He pulled out a cigarette and held it out to Van. "Here, take it."

"No, I don't want my own."

"Dude, I don't know you and I am not giving you a drag."

"I don't want a drag, I just want to stand here while you smoke."

"You just gonna stand there?"

"Yeah, and breathe."

Van closed his eyes and inhaled while the scruffy smoker exhaled a cloud of smoke. He even brought his hands up, waving the smoke toward his nose as if he were smelling the steam rising from a pot of red sauce. Marie could not let this continue. She grabbed Van's arm, pulling him away.

"Hey," he protested, looking back longingly at the boy and the smoke.

"You'll thank me later," she said and dropped his arm. She flexed her hands to get rid of the strange tingling sensation.

The tug of war that happened in Simon's office had done interesting things to her perception of

Van. He was still arrogant, but he could be fair and more stubborn than anyone she had ever met, but underneath the hot black leather jacket, the guy was seriously old-fashioned.

"How old are you, Van?" she asked as they crossed the asphalt to their cars.

"Thirty-four. Why?"

"Because, inside you are like eighty or something."

"Did you just say *like?*" he asked, stopping in his tracks. Marie stopped too and looked up at him. "How old are you, twelve?"

"Twenty-eight." She crossed her arms over her chest, ready to defend herself as she often had to when people found out about her age. She was only twenty-eight but she had done more than most people twice her age.

His mouth fell open. "You're only twenty-eight?" He was clearly floored.

"Yes, you have some sort of joke you want to make?" she challenged him.

He shook his head. "No, that's just...wow. I mean...twenty-eight?" She nodded. "That's really amazing. You've done great."

He pulled car keys out of his beat-up leather jacket and opened his door. "Twenty-eight, I can't believe it," he murmured.

Before getting in, he looked back at Marie and smiled. One of his rare full-blown smiles that changed his face completely. That sewed all of his uneven but intriguing features into what could only be called handsome.

Marie swallowed hard.

"Marie, I don't know what's going to happen, but I think it's going to be fun. See you Friday for the photo shoot." He lifted his hand in a wave, got into his sports car and drove away.

Marie walked on toward her old VW Bug, digging her keys out of her patchwork bag.

It had taken a while, but they finally agreed on ten shows. She won him over on the crabbing segment, though he had blackmailed her for that with his investigation of the best restaurant in China-town. She vetoed his Fun with Cheese because, no matter what Van said, cheese was not a full half-hour segment of fun.

She and Van were going to go to a traditional Mexican fiesta and eat all the best parts of the whole roasted pig. The best parts being the cheeks, snout and hooves. Marie couldn't wait. Van had looked truly green; for such a serious carnivore he had a limited sense of adventure. Simon wanted to do something for kids and a special Valentine's Day segment on aphrodisiacs.

She was amazed when Van agreed to a small-scale version of *Iron Chef*, and for the grand finale she and Van were going to review each other's restaurants. Simon had pushed for that one against both Van and Marie's wishes. It was bound to end in a monster fight, but Simon was the producer and, as she well knew, he had final say.

Still, despite the arguing, Van, Simon and all the rest, Marie was excited. Excited might not even be the right word. She was thrilled down to her bright red toenails.

6

Van RACED BACK to the restaurant and made sure things were running smoothly for dinner. Typically, Tuesday nights weren't big nights, but for Van there was no such thing as over-prepared. While he was cursed with bad sewage pipes, he had been more than compensated with good employees. Jack, his *sous chef*, had the kitchen cruising through prep.

"How you doing?" Van asked, patting Jack on the shoulder as he walked into the kitchen. He was immediately embraced by one of his favorite smells, garlic sautéing in olive oil. *Was there anything better?* he wondered.

"Good," Jack answered without looking up from the béchamel sauce he was making. "I didn't expect to see you today." He shot a sidelong look at Van. "Did you forget it's your day off?"

Some day off, he thought, spending the day in Simon's office with Marie was...well, it was sort of fun.

"I didn't forget." Van smiled and grabbed a

stalk of asparagus from the pile Lynn, a line chef, was preparing on the counter next to the stove.

It's a good thing I actually have something to do tonight, he thought. Everybody already gave him a hard time for working too much; he didn't need to let everyone know that he had forgotten how to do anything else.

"Well," he said, checking his watch, "I've got a few minutes before I have to leave again, I just wanted to check things out."

"Cool." Jack carefully stirred cream into his sauce.

"You ah…" Van was hovering. He knew he was hovering and hated it. *Leave, buddy, everything is fine,* he told himself, but he couldn't stop himself from asking, "You need anything? I mean I can help, or even if you needed, I could stay…"

Jack looked at Van through his slightly steamy glasses. "Get out, Van."

"Right." Van nodded feeling foolish. "I'm going." Almost reluctantly he walked through the rest of the restaurant, chewing on the asparagus as he went. With the lights on full blast in the dining room, he looked at the walls and saw deep red, but everyone from his *sous chef* to his mother had told him he was wrong. They were pink, no matter what his eyes told him. He hit the dimmer as he walked by it. Van was a firm believer in the right lighting solving most problems.

"Hey, Van." Janice, his assistant manager who

kept things running like a cruise ship, looked up from the menus she was handwriting at the bar.

The menu changed every few days at Sauvignon and so instead of printing menus he was able to just print the evening's fare on fancy stationery paper. The handwritten menus were one of the best ideas he had had for his restaurant. "What are you doing here?" Janice slipped her pen into the breast pocket of her black shirt. The staff could wear whatever they wanted, as long as it was black. Another good idea, though that was Janice's.

"Grabbing a bottle of booze. You ready for tonight?" He squeezed in behind her at the bar and opened the wine cabinet, searching for the right bottle of red.

"Van, I can do Tuesday nights in my sleep." She laughed like an old pro and Van smiled, selecting an elegant French Beaujolais.

"That's why I hired you."

He squeezed back out and headed for the door, with a certain uncomfortable anxiousness in his stomach. He tried to convince himself not to turn around, but in the end he couldn't stop himself. "I've got my cell phone if you need anything." He felt like a parent leaving his child with a babysitter for the first time.

"Out, boss. You need a night off."

"Yeah, but…"

"Out." She waved her hand at him. "We got it.

Go have your hot date, or whatever it is you're going to do with that wine."

Van fiddled for a moment with the unlit tea light on one of the tables and then left, feeling like he was leaving the better part of himself in Sauvignon.

HIS HOT DATE WAS WITH a seventy-year-old man. A seventy-year-old man with a bad attitude.

"So, you are a TV star?" Mitch Palyard, Van's friend and mentor asked as they sat down to a meal of Mitch's famous spicy mussels.

Van laughed and shook his head, though the idea sent a thrill down his backbone. "No, not yet, maybe not ever."

As Van poured the wine, he felt like his smile might actually split his face. They were eating out on Mitch's balcony so they could watch the sunset reflected across the pink-and-purple mountains that were practically in his backyard. These nights on Mitch's balcony were one of Van's very favorite things, right up there with steak and sex and old gangster films.

Van hadn't realized how tense he had been. The sudden relaxation he felt walking in the door of Mitch's home was like being high. Like the effect of morphine on pain.

The exact opposite of the day he had with Marie. It's not that time with lovely Marie was painful, far from it. It was like running at full speed for hours and not being tired. She was infuriating and invigorating all at once.

"You all right, son?" Mitch asked, his tan face lined with concern. "You're looking pale." What little white hair Mitch had left lifted off the smooth brown skin of his scalp and blew in the cool breeze. It was hard to believe, looking at the man, that he was responsible for the gourmet-food craze in the early eighties. Mitch was wearing flip-flops and an old Grateful Dead T-shirt with a hole in the armpit.

"I'm fine, Mitch."

"Good." Mitch began to dig into his mussels. "Tell me about this show of yours."

Van was actually nervous about what Mitch would say. A few days ago he had been ready to face Mitch's laughter, and maybe even laugh with him, but now after the meeting about show ideas, Van was protective of this project. It was partly his and he was beginning to like it. But as Van told him, Mitch didn't laugh once.

"Adventures in Food? That's the name?" Mitch asked and Van nodded, his mouth filled with spicy andouille sausage. "Sounds like a great idea."

"Really?" Van put down his wineglass in surprise.

"Well, I think it's a time that has come. Who wants to watch another chef roast a chicken?"

"I think if we went with roasting chicken at least once on this show, we might have a better shot at sticking around. Everyone knows that it's women who watch morning television and cooking shows and women don't eat a lot of tongue sandwiches."

Mitch laughed softly and tossed an empty shell into the big bowl that sat between the two men. "Son, what do you know about women?"

Van rolled his eyes, *Dear God, not this again*. "Mitch, just because I'm not married doesn't mean I don't know women. In fact, I would say I know women pretty well."

"Why, because you dated them?" Mitch asked. He quirked his eyebrow while sucking the juice out of a shell. "Because you've had sex with them?"

"Sure," he answered confidently. The women he dated had never complained, until he said goodbye—if that wasn't an indication, he didn't know what was.

"What's the longest relationship you've ever had?"

"Two years." With Vanessa, from cooking school in Florence. Vanessa of the endless legs and the temper and the perfect veal-stock reduction.

Mitch shook his head. "You're still wearing packaging at two years. Still playing nice."

"I've got a mother and I've got three sisters." Van was beginning to feel defensive.

Mitch started laughing so hard he choked on a piece of sausage. Van pounded the older man on the back until Mitch waved him off.

"Oh," Mitch hooted. "Oh, I haven't laughed that hard in a long time. I know your mother and sisters, Van. They worship you. They don't count." He shook his head and picked up his glass of wine.

"Then who does?" he asked, exasperated.

"How about that Marie Simmons." He let the sentence hang but lifted his eyebrows in a classic male gesture of appreciation. "Something else, that one."

The image of Marie sitting in the meeting, her skin nearly iridescent in the dim sunlight that had come in the room. Her eyes...*cool it Van,* he told himself, before he got carried away. *She's a business partner and more than a little crazy. Let's not get overexcited.*

Mitch pushed back from the table and pulled two cigars from the pocket of his jacket that was hanging over the chair. He handed one to Van.

"She's beautiful, I'll grant you that." Van reached over to light Mitch's cigar and then his own.

His nicotine-starved body nearly wept at the first taste of smoke. He wanted to eat the cigar.

"And she knows her way around her kitchen." Mitch blew a perfect smoke ring into the dark night. "I love her restaurant."

"What?" Van asked, he couldn't have been more surprised if Mitch had said he wanted to be a vegetarian. "She makes salads and things with chocolate chips—she might as well be fast food."

"Such snobbery in one so young..." Mitch tsk-tsked his tongue.

"You're the one who told me that you could tell just by one taste how long someone worked on their consommé. You're the one who said anything worth learning was worth learning right."

"Well, I didn't say it first, but I think it applies to cooking. The question is why don't you think it applies to Marie?"

"Because I don't think she's taken much time to learn anything about cooking." Van shrugged and rolled his cigar in his mouth, appreciating every moment of the contraband tobacco. "I think she's all style and no substance."

"And you sadly are all substance and not a single ounce of style." Mitch smiled and stretched out his legs. "I think she's going to surprise you, Van."

"Oh, she surprises me all the time," Van admitted. "But I don't think it's going to change my opinion of her."

"You want to sleep with her?" Mitch asked with a very not-seventy-year-old twinkle in his eyes.

"I haven't given it much thought," Van lied, unable to look Mitch in the eye.

"Well, don't." Mitch waved his cigar at him. "Nothing ruins a professional relationship like romance."

Van looked at Mitch askance. "Didn't you marry your *sous chef*?"

"Yep." Mitch nodded emphatically. "Susanne and I got married and the restaurant went bankrupt. I had to start all over again and I never found a *sous chef* to compare."

"Yeah, but you found a wife." Whenever they talked about Susanne, Van felt the soft trembling nature of the subject. Mitch rarely talked about his wife, who died of cancer three years ago.

Mitch nodded with a sad smile. "But she was a very good *sous chef.*"

"And as a wife?"

Mitch leaned his head back and Van noticed that the stars were coming out, bright pinpoints against a violet sky. The silence went on so long Van guessed Mitch wasn't going to answer. Van would allow the man his privacy. He practiced his smoke rings.

"Every man should be blessed with a woman like that," Mitch said. He examined the glowing end of his cigar and Van felt his whole body go tense, like he was getting ready to take a punch. "She was like a queen. My queen."

Van let out a soft sigh of air. He wanted a family, a woman who could be a queen. Marie, and the way she walked and carried herself, the way she fought for her ideas at the meeting and went toe-to-toe with him at every opportunity, popped into his mind, but he shook the image of her out of his head.

Partners, nothing more.

"LOOK I'LL WEAR POWDER, I understand I need powder but I am drawing the line at mascara." Van held up his hands, trying to fend off the makeup ladies. Nobody ever said anything about mascara, or lipstick, when they talked about the photo shoot. Somebody should have warned him.

"Van, those eyebrows make your eyes practically disappear. We've got to do something or you're going to be all eyebrows in the picture." Teresa, who looked like she could wrestle him to the ground if she needed to, came at him again, brandishing the mascara wand. Van dodged right and stepped out of her way.

He couldn't believe it, but he looked at Marie for help. Since this whole photo shoot started, she had been nothing but calm and rational and quite successful at fending off Teresa and her minions.

It was awkward being in a position of gratitude to the woman since he came in this morning ready to do battle with her.

"Let's take a few shots with the digital without the makeup and see what he thinks." Marie said, holding perfectly still while Teresa's assistant did her makeup. She sounded like an old pro and Van wondered if maybe he wasn't a little wrong about her. Maybe she wasn't sent by the devil to cause him grief.

Teresa blew her bangs off her forehead and shrugged. "Whatever." She walked away and Van, chagrined, smiled his thanks at Marie.

They were in a photographer's studio that was actually not too far from their restaurants, in one of the warehouses in the area. Both Marie and Van had come with food—he brought homemade smoked salmon that tasted like heaven on her savory rosemary-and-thyme scones.

Music by Coldplay was being pumped in and everyone was in a pretty relaxed and energetic mood. Except Van. He went to run his fingers through his hair but all the hair spray made it impossible.

Mascara. Costumes. Teresa actually wanted to pluck his eyebrows. It was all so very foreign to him. Perhaps the strangest thing was the fact that Marie was his guide and she hadn't led him into a single ambush.

"Hey, guys!" Simon, all smiles came in and shook hands before handing some papers to Van and Marie.

"We've got a preliminary script for the first episode. We're going with the favorite restaurant in Chinatown." Van wanted to gloat that his idea had been picked first, but refrained.

"We're going to tape Sunday night." Simon continued, "Since your slot is going to be on Tuesday mornings, that gives us time to mix and fix on Mondays. So some weeks we're going to need you Sundays, sometimes on Monday and Tuesday mornings. Next week we need you Friday morning to do a live interview on the show and we will tape Sunday night."

"Simon, you've got to be kidding," Marie

turned away from the girl doing her makeup. "We've got restaurants to run. Can't we try and tighten this up…." She looked to Van for help, and while he didn't have a problem, he nodded in agreement because he felt he owed her for scaring away Teresa.

Simon shrugged. "It's a short bit Monday morning and a couple of hours Sunday night to be taped for Tuesday's show. It's a weekly show, Marie. That's the kind of schedule we keep."

After a moment Marie put a smile on her face that Van could tell was forced. "Who needs sleep?" she joked and Van inwardly winced. A baker's hours were tough and finding help for early morning was harder than night staff. Van felt a stab of sympathy for Marie.

"So," Simon said, "we're splitting the show into thirds. A little history about Chinatown, then we go to Van's favorite place and then Marie's. But for the last third we've added a little something special." Behind his glasses, his eyes were absolutely devilish.

That scares me, Van thought and flipped quickly through the script to the end.

"What a great idea, Simon!" Marie cried, having arrived at the special ending first.

Van scanned the pages, his stomach in his feet. If Marie thought it was a great idea, Van could guarantee he would hate it.

One-Hundred-Year-Old Chinese Eggs. They

were going to eat them. It was well known among people who cared that one-hundred-year-old Chinese eggs were one of the vilest things ever created by cooks.

"We're going to have to eat one?" he asked, swallowing the sour taste that immediately sprang to the back of his throat.

"You're going to have to try." Simon rubbed his hands together. "Now, the script is really loose, lots of room for improv. But—" Simon took a few steps to the right to check the progress on the photo set "—I think we've got time. I want to do a quick rehearsal, see how the script reads for you guys."

Van broke out in a cold sweat. "Right now?"

"Now's good." Simon nodded.

"But…" He expected having a lot more time with the script before having to read anything out loud. Time to memorize, watch himself in the mirror, practice his moves.

"It's okay, Van." Marie put a hand on his arm. "We just read it, no big deal."

Easy for you to say, Van thought, trying to calm the pterodactyl-sized butterflies in his stomach.

"From the top," Simon said and crossed his arms over his chest.

"That means the beginning," Marie whispered. Van shot her a quelling look. He was new, not stupid.

She started talking about the history of Chinatown in such a natural and relaxed way that Van couldn't believe she was actually reading from a script. He glanced up from the words to make sure she was. Admiration curled through him, surprising the hell out of him.

"Van?" She was looking at him. Those big blue eyes were warm and kind. She wasn't so bad....

"Earth to Van?" She snapped her fingers in front of his face. "Stay with us."

"Sorry." He looked back down at his script, picked up his part and read, trying to inject his voice with the same loose, casual tone that Marie had. He thought it was going pretty well, maybe too fast. *Am I breathing too much?* He tried to breathe a little less but that didn't work either. So he decided not to worry about it.

"Good food should be an adventure" was his last line. He caught Marie's eye as she said hers, "Come on, I dare you."

Well, he thought, *that wasn't so hard.* He looked at Simon, who was watching them silently. *Uh-oh.* He glanced back at Marie who was beaming.

"This is going to be huge." Simon threw his hands in the air. "Huge!"

"We're ready!" the photographer yelled.

"So, it was okay?" Van asked.

"You were great, Van. Really, really good," Marie told him, shaking her head like she couldn't quite believe it. "Let's go get our picture taken."

7

THE FOLLOWING WEDNESDAY afternoon Marie lifted the door to her ancient industrial dishwasher. *Please let this work.* The gods of used kitchen appliances had been pretty good to her so far, considering this dishwasher should have been put in a scrap heap before she bought it. But she had the sinking suspicion that her luck was running out.

She waited exactly two Mississippis and then brought the door slamming down with a metallic bang. She followed this with a small half lift of the door before gently bringing it back down.

"Anything?" She asked Pete, who was crouched behind the ancient dishwasher with various pliers and wrenches and other useless tools.

Pete shook his head.

"Worked last time." Marie's last-ditch effort was to spit in her hand and slam the side of the old equipment, giving its mechanical innards a good shaking.

Nothing but the dead silence of a broken dishwasher.

"It's toast, isn't it?" Marie asked and Pete nodded. He stood up and shrugged.

"Thanks, Pete," she whispered, suddenly feeling as if she might cry. She rubbed her gritty, tired eyes. Van had stopped the live music so she should be sleeping better, only now she was plagued by dreams of pirates who smelled like rosemary and garlic.

"I'm leaving early today," Pete reminded her. She nodded, scared to talk because of the lump in her throat. He walked past her, back into the dining room.

I want to leave early, too, her inner child whined.

Marie walked over to the stove and turned off the burners underneath pots of boiling water and carrot-ginger soup before going outside for some perspective and fresh air in her herb garden. The dishwasher wasn't a surprise. She was amazed it had held up this long.

She used both hands to push open the door and stepped into the small area under the steps that served as a staff lounge, herb garden and slipshod refuge. With the rain dripping off the gutters, it was almost like a fountain.

Her herbs smelled great in the cool wet weather. She picked a sprig of mint and crushed it between her fingers as she sat down in one of the two chairs Jodi and Pete had set up.

Because of the hours at *AMSF* she was going to have to hire two new staff members and now she needed to get the new dishwasher she had been putting off for a month, without any real delivery of that promise of extra income coming in. And she still hadn't found a baker.

She was exhausted. And with her defenses down, the doubts that she constantly had to fight off came buzzing around like angry bees. *Why are you even bothering here, Marie? You could go and get a job working for someone else. Take the pressure off yourself. What are you trying to prove? You know you're just going to leave anyway. If not now, then later.*

The voice in her head was her mother's. The woman Marie was so scared she was going to turn into.

These thoughts would get her nowhere; they certainly wouldn't get her any closer to a new dishwasher. *You're just tired and a little lonely.*

She tried to conjure up something good beneath her eyelids, but all of the sunsets and beaches and mountains and bazaars she had seen felt so far away.

"Well, well, hello partner."

"Go away," Marie told Van without opening her eyes. "Seriously."

"Pleasant as usual, I see." Van sat, one hundred percent uninvited, in the seat opposite her next to her boxed-in herb garden. Her eyes flew open. "You can grow Thai basil back here?" he asked and bent over her herbs, manhandling her basil. "I get too much sunlight." He picked a deep purple leaf, crushed it in his hand and smelled it. He turned to her with a look that was somehow as earthy as her plants. Marie recoiled at the tiny fissure of warmth in her bloodstream.

Oh, no, you don't. Not this guy, she told herself. He had somehow wormed his way past all of her righteous anger at the photo shoot. His obvious bafflement had hit her right in her soft spot and she found herself in the strange position of taking Van under her wing. And, even stranger, he seemed to appreciate it.

Van sniffed the herb again and then dropped it back onto the black soil of her garden. The small space under the stairs was suddenly intimate, as if his laugh and his presence had an effect on the distance between them. He was feet away from her but she could feel him, as if he were beside her.

"Van?" she said, too tired to put up a good fight. "Not that I don't just love your uninvited presence in my herb garden, but what do you want?"

Van leaned over in his seat to pull something out of the back pocket of his pin-striped black chef pants.

With a flourish, he unfolded a torn out page from a magazine and another one from a newspaper. "Did you see the paper today, or the new *Where* magazine?"

"No." Marie leaned forward and reached for the paper but he pulled it away. He unfolded the page and showed it to her. What she saw were ads for the show. Big type across the top of the page that copied the Indiana Jones movie type declared: Food Meets Adventure on *AMSF*.

The picture was of Van and Marie standing back to back. He was wearing his signature black chef's jacket with the red lettering on the breast, but he was also wearing a beat-up brown fedora.

Marie was wearing a white chef's jacket with Marie's Bistro embroidered in periwinkle-blue above her trademark stylized tulip. She was holding a bullwhip and wearing a little too much blush.

"I can't believe it!" Her bad mood and money worries vanished in the thrill of seeing the ad.

"Yeah, I know. It's amazing, isn't it? I can't believe that picture turned out." He leaned back and this time perused her herb garden before picking a sprig of lemon balm and putting it in his mouth to chew.

Marie examined the photo. Van looked perfect. His sharp features were subdued by the half curve of his lips and the twinkle in his eyes. And of course the hat. There weren't that many men in the world who could carry that look and Van did it with class and charm. He looked like an invitation to trouble; women across the city were going to love it. "You look great," she said honestly.

Van laughed again, his eyes on her face, which made her very aware of how tired she looked.

"You, as usual, look gorgeous." For a moment Marie couldn't do anything but breath and let herself get wrapped up in his gaze.

"Of course, right now you look like death." He turned back to graze from her herb garden, pulling up a piece of parsley and popping it in his mouth.

"Screw you Van, and stop eating my herbs," she snapped, furious at herself for being suckered in by his sudden nice-guy disguise.

"Hey, hey, I'm just kidding." Van did the impossible, the unbelievable; he put his hand on her shoulder. The heat of it, the feel of his palm touching her, the brush of his thumb across the exposed skin at the top of her neck made her eyes heavy.

"What are you doing right now?" he asked and Marie tried not to notice the trouble shining in his eyes. But it was impossible. She smiled back. She always was a sucker for a guy with trouble on his mind.

"Besides contemplating life selling oranges to tourists? I'm cooking some soup."

Van checked his watch, stood and strolled into her kitchen through the back door.

"Hey," she cried, running after him.

"Ah, no wonder you're in a bad mood. Your dishwasher's busted." He tsk-tsked and Marie stepped around him to give him hell. Who goes barging into someone else's kitchen?

"Can I help you?" Jodi asked in an arch tone that made Marie proud. She was standing next to Pete at one of the work spaces as they rolled cutlery in napkins.

"Yeah, Van, what's the—"

"Is it a big deal if Marie leaves for about an hour and a half?" Van asked and both Pete and Jodi's mouths fell open.

Jodi started to smirk. "What are you going to do?"

"Nothing!" Marie cried. "Because I am not going." But part of her was already out the door.

"You guys are about to close, right?" Van asked.

Jodi and Pete nodded in unison.

"Van, I was in the middle of making soup."

"I can finish the soup." Pete volunteered and Marie was so surprised that she just stared at him dumbfounded. Her quiet, dreadlocked barista wanted to make soup? "Carrot-ginger, right?" Pete shook a dreadlock out of his eyes. "I can do that."

"I thought you had to leave early?" Marie asked. Pete and Jodi shared a quick look and Pete finally shrugged.

"It's cool."

"See, if the guy says it's cool, it's cool. Let's go." Van turned to her. "In an hour and a half, you can come back and do whatever you need to do."

"You can cook?" Marie asked Pete.

"He's a great cook," Jodi piped up and Pete blushed, shuffling his feet. Jodi shooed her hands at Marie, behind Van's back. "Go," she mouthed, "go-go-go."

"Come on," Van chuckled and Marie's stomach

tightened in response to the low rumbly bass coming from his chest. He grabbed her hand and led her back outside. "I'm taking you on a field trip."

Marie stared dumbly at her hand in his. She could feel the calluses on the pads of his fingers and he had a small, almost healed, cut along his palm. His skin was dry, rough almost, but so warm and the temptation to leave her hand there in his big palm was almost overwhelming.

She pulled her hand loose.

She'd go on this field trip, but she wouldn't hold his hand. It sounded reasonable to her.

Twenty minutes later, out of town and in a whole different weather system, Van and Marie parked on a small side street. It wasn't exactly sunny, but at least it wasn't raining.

"You said this was a secret beach," Marie said as they made their way across the street toward the sand and ocean.

"Any beach in the middle of a day you should be working feels like a secret beach."

Marie couldn't argue with that logic since she felt like a schoolkid playing hooky.

Van kicked off his chef clogs and removed his socks, and Marie tried not to stare at his feet. But they were remarkably handsome. Marie slid off her own clogs and quickly tried to hide her mismatched socks.

"You color-blind?" Van asked.

"No." Marie put her one purple sock and one

red sock in her pockets. "Just tired at three in the morning."

"Three in the morning?" Van asked and Marie nodded. She picked up a shiny piece of blue glass that was in her path and put it in her pocket. She had a nice collection of beach glass from around the world on her kitchen windowsill. "No wonder you were asleep in the car. Three in the morning is a crime, Marie, a real crime."

"You're telling me," she laughed. "Sometimes I have no idea what made me do this."

"Do what? Marie's Bistro?" he asked.

"Yeah, Marie's Bistro. The twenty-hour days can make you crazy." Marie slid a little in the deep sand, off balance. Van grabbed her elbow and pulled her upright. She ignored the electrical zing that shimmied up her arm.

"It's supposed to get better," Van said hopefully. She shot an incredulous look at him. "That's what I've heard anyway." He shrugged. "I don't mind it so much. Long days, longer nights. No vacation. I'll take it."

Tell me that in another six months, she thought but remained silent because it seemed like they were being nice to each other.

"Well, I've always thought you were crazy," she said instead.

"You must be, too," Van rejoined. "This life isn't for the weak of heart."

"No, it really isn't," Marie agreed, but she was

a total fraud. An hour ago she was ready to walk away. If that wasn't faint of heart she didn't know what was. "You always want to be a chef?"

"Yep," Van answered almost before she finished asking the question. "Always. Well, after the astronaut phase."

"Of course." Marie nodded solemnly.

"My mom went back to work when I was about eight," Van said, slipping his hands into his pockets. "So my sisters and I would come home from school and the woman next door would come over and sit with us until Mom came home. The woman was Susanne Palyard, Mitch Palyard's wife."

"Get out," she breathed. Mitch Palyard was only the most respected and revered chef on the West Coast, perhaps both coasts. His book of recipes and anecdotes and travel tips—*The World Table*—was one of the few things she carried around the globe.

"It's the truth. She and Mitch couldn't have children and so my sisters and I sort of became their honorary kids."

"Did Mitch teach you to cook?"

"Hell, no," Van laughed. "The man couldn't teach anyone how to boil water. Susanne taught me. Mitch mentored me. It was..." He paused looking up at the sky for the right word.

Marie, in what was a very strange moment for her, felt a little humbled by Van.

"Sounds wonderful," she supplied with a shy smile.

"You could say that," he said and continued across the sand, his long strides outdistancing her. "You could also say it was a very specific kind of torture. Mitch is sort of an acquired taste."

She chuckled and they fell into a companionable silence that gave Marie a chance to realize how incredibly out of shape she was. She tried not to pant for air.

Van suddenly bent his knees and collapsed onto a sand dune.

"Man, I am out of shape," Van panted. "Let's just sit here. We both know that water is cold." Van squinted up at her pleadingly and so she gladly fell down next to him.

Marie burrowed her toes in the cool sand. She watched the endless roll of the ocean and felt enormously grateful to Van for bringing her here.

"Have you always lived in San Francisco?" Marie asked, grabbing handfuls of the sand and letting it run through her fingers. She felt her stress and bad mood trickle away.

"Nope." Van picked up a frayed stick and twirled it. "I went to cooking school in Italy and worked for a while in France...."

"Where in France?" Marie asked. She had spent two years there, falling in love with food and cooking—and Ian.

"Cannes," Van answered.

"Oh, the red cliffs of the Esterel." Marie smiled at the visual memory of the stunning cliffs along the coast of France. "I worked at Le Papillon," Marie told Van, tooting her own horn because she could. Not everyone worked at Le Papillon.

"Under Gerard Renaud?" He was clearly impressed. Le Papillon was the most exclusive restaurant in Cannes.

"Sadly, yes." She laughed remembering the little Napoleon, who for six months had it out for her. "I almost ended up in jail, he was so infuriating."

"I heard one of his line chefs threw a knife at him."

"That would be me." She wasn't one hundred percent proud of that but part of her still wished she had winged the arrogant bastard. "Where were you in Italy?"

"I studied at Académie Cordon Bleu."

"Well, look at you Mr. Hotshot." Van lifted his shoulder in a not-so-humble shrug

"When did you go to school?" he asked, shifting so he was cross-legged. His knee pressed against hers and she left it there, because it felt warm and solid and good.

"I didn't," she said, shrugging. "I mean I've taken some classes but you know, almost wherever you go restaurants will hire people under the table, so I've worked my way up in kitchens all over the world. Ireland, Spain, France, Vietnam." She grinned at Van and then went back to her careful consideration of sand. She was stepping pretty casually right into friendly, intimate conversation with this guy. The last thing she needed was to get caught up in those eyes of his. "By the time I got to Gerard, I had enough recommendations to land me in his kitchen."

Van was studying her, like a puzzle he couldn't quite figure out. "You know, Marie, if you had told me that a week ago I probably would have nodded and told you I could tell." He shook his head. "I hate to admit it, but I would have thought less of you."

"And now?" she asked, baffled that she even cared what he thought.

He took a deep breath. "I can't believe I am saying this but I think I admire you more."

Marie didn't know what to say. She barely knew how to feel. Part of her was inordinately pleased and flattered that she had managed to impress this man. The other half screamed *run*.

The space between them filled with opportunity and desire.

She knew that if she turned toward him, if she met his eyes, they would kiss. He would look genuinely amazed by her, while at the same time heartbreakingly attractive with the wind in his hair. He would smile, or maybe she would, and they would slowly lean in toward each other until their lips touched.

It was one of those moments that with another

man she would take full advantage of. She would rush headlong right into whatever might happen on the sand.

Lord knows I could use a little rolling around in the sand.

But not with him. And resisting him was harder than she ever dreamed.

He finally looked away, his head turned toward the far rocks out in the water. "Sometimes, Marie, I just don't know what to say to you."

She nodded, and kicked the sand, feeling empty pretending not to want him. "I kind of like it that way."

With Van focused on the far rocks, Marie turned to him and foolishly looked him over. She watched his silver-and-black hair lift and wave in the wind coming off the ocean. She wanted to touch it, run it through her fingers.

She felt a low shift in her belly, a warning of sorts and she looked away.

Run now! The adult in her was getting tired of being ignored. But she didn't run. Nope, she stayed. And more than just staying, she ignored all the conflicting impulses ricocheting through her body and took the opportunity to lie back in the sand.

She put her hands under her head and just let herself be. She refused to think about Van, the dishwasher, about the TV show, about how early tomorrow morning might come, all of it. She was a woman on a beach, with roughly twenty-five more minutes off; she was with a sort-of-nice man, and the sun was shining a little bit. It was enough. She sighed and let herself be happy.

"Marie?"

"Hmm…" Marie hummed.

"Are we becoming friends?" he asked and the question pierced something inside of her, and she suddenly felt all too aware of the fragile nature of her heart and the recklessness with which she always seemed to throw it in harm's way.

She reached out and tapped his hand. "Let's just be quiet." Van chuckled softly, patted her hand back and she could sense in the shifting of air and sand that he had lain down next to her. His hand, like the dim sunlight and sea air, was still resting on hers.

8

FRIDAY MORNING SIMON LED Van and Marie through the maze-like inner workings of *AMSF.*

This is it! This is it! This is it! Marie chanted in time to her heels hitting the cement floor. She couldn't wipe the grin off her face or lose the urge she had to hug the whole world. Today was the day she built the second floor of her empire.

"It's disgusting how awake you are," Van said between yawns that looked like they were going to split his face.

"I've been awake since three, Van. Remember?"

"Disgusting," he muttered.

Already this morning, Marie had proofed her dough and gotten things started for Jodi, who had agreed to come in early. And truly, the coup de grâce for the day, she managed to find the only clean pair of tights left in her drawer. They were black-and-gray plaid, and she thought they added a nice touch to her knee-length black suede skirt and the burgandy V-neck shirt she was wearing.

"Okay," Simon whispered as they stood in the

wings of the *AMSF* set. The hosts were chatting onstage about the latest *New York Times* bestseller, both pretending to have read it when Marie knew that they hadn't. They couldn't read a word unless it came up on a teleprompter.

Rick Anderson, a fifty-year-old former game-show host, and Luanne Edwin, a former beauty queen who, despite being forty years old, had lost none of her looks thanks to the magic of collagen, sat behind a high counter on comfortable stools, as if they were in someone's kitchen. They had coffee cups at their sides, bland artwork and flowers behind them; they could have been in any suburban breakfast nook.

"Luanne and Rick are going to introduce you two and you are going to go out there and answer some questions. It's an eight-minute segment, so don't get too long-winded," Simon told them. Van and Marie both nodded, and then Van yawned.

"And don't yawn," Simon whispered.

Onstage, Luanne laughed at something Rick had said. She leaned her blond head on Rick's shoulder, weak with laughter and the audience started to clap. *Oh brother,* Marie rolled her eyes at Van, who managed to smile, despite the fact that he was beginning to look a little nervous.

Rick signed them off to go to a commercial and the red lights on the cameras went out and the stage was no longer live.

"Kill mics," Luanne purred to the producers in

the booth and as soon as the mics were dead she turned on Rick like a rabid dog.

"You're an idiot." Van's head snapped back at Luanne's tone, and Marie remembered just how ugly it was the first time she witnessed the co-hosts turn on each other.

"And you're getting old," Rick growled. People ran up to the hosts to reapply makeup but Rick and Luanne kept up the bickering.

"You're stepping all over my lines." Luanne lifted her chin and closed her eyes while her blond hair was resprayed into submission.

"Yeah, because you're delivering them like a donkey," Rick spat while getting rouged and powdered.

"Ten seconds people," a producer shouted. Cameras moved and music was cued. "Five seconds."

"We've got a shadow on three, somebody get that!" a woman with three pens in her hair and murder in her eyes screamed as she ran past Marie and Van.

"It's three, two…"

"I think I'm going to be sick," Van whispered.

"Don't you dare, Van. Come on, toughen up," Marie whispered. She took his hand in hers and gave it a little shake. And then, because it was cold and clammy, she gave it a squeeze. They were partners in this and suddenly Marie felt a sense of team spirit.

So what if he was arrogant? So what if she wanted very badly to see the man naked? She could get over that for the sake of the greater good. That good being the empire. They were a team and that was all that mattered.

She didn't know when it happened. But things had changed for her. He wasn't quite a friend but he was no longer the enemy.

"You're going to be fine," Marie said and stepped up to the big man to hug him. She wrapped her arms around his shoulders and felt his hands come up to her back and it was like hugging an electrical current. From the tips of her fingers to her breasts to the suddenly powerful ache between her legs, she could feel him.

"Marie…?" he breathed into her hair. His hands running down her back, his thumb tracing the curve of her spine.

This isn't the way to go about building team spirit, Marie told herself, trying to get a grip on what was happening to her.

She quickly pulled away, smiled as if things weren't more than just a little confusing between them and turned around to watch the action on the stage.

"Hi everyone and welcome back to the show," Luanne said brightly, crossing her thin legs.

"Well, the producers here at *AMSF* have done it again," Rick said in his friendly baritone.

"They sure have, Rick." Luanne cut in and Marie saw the looks being thrown around backstage. Luanne was having one of her diva days, which at best meant she was unpredictable and vicious, and at worse it meant she would eat her own children to get more camera time. It was shaping up to be a bad first day for Van.

Marie darted a look at Van from the corner of her eye and the way he was sort of freaking out was very endearing to her.

No hugging, Marie.

She crossed her arms and bumped him with her hip. "Think calming thoughts," she told him.

"Shut up Marie, or I'll puke on you."

"The folks here at *AMSF* are going to redefine cooking shows." Rick pressed on, trying to stick to the script. "Van MacAllister, chef and owner of Sauvignon—have you been there yet, Luanne?" Rick asked.

"No," she answered flatly, batting her eyes. Both Marie and Van cringed.

"She was there last week," Van whispered into Marie's left ear, and the left side of her body lit up like a flambé. "She hit on me."

"Shut up."

"I'm not kidding. She left her phone number on a matchbook. Very classy." He waggled his eyebrows but still looked a little white. And sweaty.

"Wipe your face, Van. You look like a junkie." Van blotted his face with his sleeve. Marie snagged a makeup girl who quickly applied powder to him.

"I took my wife there for dinner two nights ago and she hasn't shut up about this man and his

food since. Giovanni MacAllister is the hottest
thing to hit San Francisco dining since…I don't
know, fire," Rick said.

There was some polite laughing from the live
audience and Van groaned and put his head in
his hands.

"Well, we all know Marie from right here on
AMSF," Luanne rallied, getting back on the script.
"She has been our regular foodie for a few months
now and for those of you who haven't gotten to
her restaurant, shame on you. Because I don't
know what Marie Simmons is doing in that little
kitchen of hers, but it's magic."

"Well, hopefully they'll be making some magic
on this show. They are going to be taking the very
best that San Francisco has to offer and they are
going to turn it on its head. Or its stomach," Rick
added and Luanne laughed and laughed, resting
her forehead on his shoulder. Rick looked out into
the audience and shrugged as if his incredible wit
and the control it had over the old beauty queen
were just beyond him.

"Let's bring them out here, folks, Marie Simmons and Van MacAllister."

"Here we go Van," she whispered. They
walked onto the stage, under the bright lights that
were hotter than her kitchen during Sunday
brunch. The crowd cheered and Marie could see
the shiny new dishwasher in a matter of weeks.

Van tried not to squint into the light. They told

him not to, but they never said it would be so bright. And the red lights on the camera, were those things on? All four of them?

His stomach rolled and he swallowed hard.

Whatever you do, don't throw up on live TV.

Van became very aware of the size of his nose and the possible shadow it could be casting on the rest of the set. He tried to angle himself so that three of the four cameras would at least have his good side, but that made him angle away from the action and Marie put a hand on his arm.

She's talking to me, Van thought, but he was just…it was those lights. The little red ones. How many people could possibly be watching right now? His mom was. He knew that. Mitch probably.

"Van?" It was Marie, trying to talk to him. She dug her fingernails into his leg like an angry cat and he turned his head to look at her.

"Aren't you thrilled about the show?" Her smile was bright but her eyes were completely pissed off and the nails were digging deeper.

Van ducked his chin to his chest to better talk into the little microphone that was pinned to the lapel of his chef's jacket.

"Yes," he said. "I am thrilled about the show."

Marie's smile vanished and for a moment she looked as horrified as he should feel. He felt like he was watching everything from under water and in slow motion.

The crazy female producer was mouthing

something at him from off stage but there was a dull roar in his ears and the heavy throb of his heartbeat.

He felt sweat rolling down the side of his face in a trickle.

"Which one are you most excited about?" Marie asked through her teeth.

"I'm excited about It Tastes Like Chicken," he said, this time keeping his chin up. But he knew it was bad. It was those lights, the red ones. He could see them out of the corner of his eye. Marie nodded, but looked at him like she was watching a little kid pull down his pants at the talent show.

She turned to continue to talk to the hosts, leaving him for dead behind her.

Calming thoughts, think calming thoughts.

He blinked, shook his head and thought of a glass of Shiraz and a perfectly grilled lamb shank with oven-roasted tomatoes. A Keith's Pale Ale and a bacon cheeseburger with blue cheese. *Calming. Calming thoughts. Breathe Van. Breathe.*

"Van, why are people going to want to watch you? Other than your obvious appeal to the women," Luanne cooed.

"I think what we're doing is different. I've never seen anything like it on TV," he said and he could see Marie's shoulders relax. "Mostly, though," he continued, imagining Guinness and lightly fried pierogies, "I think it's going to be fun watching you eat pig snout, Marie."

"Oh, Van who are you kidding? I love pig snout."

"Mark my words." Van even managed to look out at the camera. "One look at hairy, black barbecued pig snout and it's going to be all over for Marie."

"We'll see, Van. We'll see."

Van thought that he could actually taste and smell the electricity between them it was so thick. When he put his hand on her shoulder, his thumb landed above the collar of her clingy red shirt on the soft skin of her neck.

Suddenly instead of food and drink he imagined Marie and her long black hair, her full gypsy mouth, her breasts that pressed against everything she wore. Even with the red lights gleaming in the side of his vision, the world narrowed and dimmed until it was just him and Marie. He left his hand on her, his thumb gently stroking that skin.

Marie's look was warm and he got lost in the wild blue of those eyes. Her lips parted and their breath came in at the same time. It only lasted maybe half a second but all he could feel was the skin of her neck and the hard beating of her heart beneath it.

"Oh, that sounds like a challenge," Rick said with a laugh, rubbing his hands together. Marie blinked and looked back at the hosts, subtly pulling away from Van's hand. He let it drop.

That had been a mistake. He felt burned, singed by the chemistry between them.

"Who are you putting your money on, Jimmy?" Rick asked.

The cameraman quickly pointed to Marie and everyone laughed.

"It's always a safe bet putting your money on the woman," Luanne cooed, batting her eyes at Rick, who groaned.

"Don't I know it." The crowd laughed again. "We'll be right back with a performance by Isho Tamaki, the winner of *Japanese Idol*."

"I can't wait." Luanne clapped her hands and the little red lights on the cameras went off and Van sucked in air like a drowning man.

"Oh my God, Van!" Marie slid off her stool and hauled him off his, running for backstage. "Stage fright! Was that a joke?"

"'Fraid not," he muttered, shaking off the underwater feeling. They both ducked as two men lifted cables over their heads.

"You have got to get over that." Marie's eyes were flashing and Van, off balance, remembered the endlessness of the look she gave him out there, the downy softness of her skin. *This is trouble. More trouble than stage fright.*

"Okay," Simon whispered, nodding his head as he came over to them. "That could have been worse."

"How?" Marie snapped, her voice climbing out of a whisper. "How could that have been worse?"

"I could have thrown up."

"Not funny."

No, he didn't think so, either.

"What happened, Van? You were great during rehearsal."

He could only shrug. During rehearsal there were none of those little red lights around.

"We can't do a whole show like that." Marie turned to Simon. "We looked like idiots."

"Actually—" Simon shook his head "—the last little bit was pretty great. Once Van joined the living you guys had a lot of chemistry." Simon broke into a smile, his face shiny in the dark light backstage. "Food, adventure and sex. We're going to have a great show."

Simon chased after the woman with the pens in her hair, and Van and Marie were left staring at each other.

Sex. Someone else said it. Someone else noticed it. It wasn't just something between them. He looked at her—her blue eyes wide and knowing and wished that she were a different person. Not a chef, not a competitor and not his business partner.

"Heads up!" someone whispered and Van pulled Marie out of the way as two men trotted past them carrying a spotlight.

"Thanks," she breathed, her hand on his chest. The smell of her, herbs and lemon, lifted off her hair and wrapped around him.

He had a devil in him, that's what his mother always said, and when Marie pulled away, the devil in Van pulled her closer. Marie's eyes lifted to his and while he expected a lot of things—coyness, surprise, anger—he was amazed by the frank and answering desire he saw reflected there.

She wanted him, too.

9

VAN'S HAND FLEXED ON HER ARM and Marie stood there absorbing the heat and energy that was Giovanni MacAllister.

She felt his breath against her cheek and slid right into the bottomless black pools of his eyes. *Hey!* The adult Marie who was not moved by this man and raging hormones tried to take over.

But Marie ignored her. Her lips parted and her body swayed minutely toward him. She took a deep breath, inhaling mint and the moody spicy scent that was all Van, and her breasts touched his chest. *Oh boy*, Marie thought. *Oh boy.*

"You're trouble, Van," Marie whispered, her mouth kicking up in the corner. "And I think that's what I like about you."

"I could say the same about you," Van murmured. Marie held her breath, not wanting to be the one to make this move, to change this relationship, to open this Pandora's box. But at the same time, she wanted it, so very badly. Bad enough to stand there, Van's eyes on her mouth, and to wish that he would just bend down a fraction of an inch and make the suddenly painful longing blooming inside of her go away.

"Coming through," someone whispered rushing by with an armful of pillows. She and Van jumped apart like guilty teenagers.

"I…ah," he said, and stopped. His hand came up to the scar on his chin, his telling gesture of nerves, which made him infinitely more attractive at that moment.

"Yes, I ah…" She trailed off too, examining the toes of her boots. She was choked by the million unsaid things she should be saying. *Sorry, can't do it. Sorry, you're my business partner. Sorry, I'm on hiatus from overcomplicated relationships.* All of those would have been acceptable. She was struck dumb by the haywire impulses her body was sending out. She, Marie Simmons, was losing her cool. So instead she said, "I need to get back to the restaurant. Yeah, I gotta go."

She turned and walked away and fought the urge to look back to see if he was watching her.

SUNDAY NIGHT VAN AND MARIE were shivering on a busy street corner in Chinatown. He was wearing his world-traveler leather coat and Marie had her favorite quilted red silk Chinese jacket on. Incredibly stylish, yes, but not much good against the sharp wind whistling up the hills and through the streets of Chinatown.

"I…come on…do I have to wear this?" Van whined while Teresa applied mascara to his long eyelashes. "Food, adventure and sex, I can't be sexy with mascara on."

Oh, yes you can, Marie thought, parts of her body still reeling from the near-kiss a few days ago.

Another makeup artist held up a mirror and Marie checked out her reflection and nodded. Her black hair was pulled back into a tight bun that made her eyes large and her jawline a little tighter. Van and Teresa made a working compromise on the issue of blush and they were ready to go.

Ready to go, ha! Marie pressed a hand to the butterflies that were whirling in her stomach.

After the fiasco on Friday morning, there was no telling how the taping was going to go. She quickly glanced at Van to see if he looked like he was going to be sick.

He did.

Great! Just great! My cooking empire is tied to a guy with stage fright.

"All right, here's what's happening folks." The woman with three pens in her hair, whose name Marie had learned was Agnes, approached them from behind the cameraman. "We're walking and talking, you guys gab about Chinese immigrants and ducks in windows, whatever you want. When you get to here—" she stopped at a crack in the sidewalk beside a small Chinese junk shop with a plethora of red lanterns spilling from its doors "—you stop. Any questions?"

"Yeah," Van said. "Do those cameras have those red lights on them like the ones in the studio?"

Agnes furrowed her brow. "No."

"Then let's get this show on the road." Van shot Marie a wide smile. His about-to-be-sick look was gone. Marie steeled herself against the rush of feelings he inspired in her. After the near-kiss on Friday, she was resolute to get things back on firmer ground. They were business partners. Nothing more. These oddball impulses about touching him and hugging him and wanting to take his clothes off, they were useless. These feelings had nowhere to go.

He slung his arm around her shoulder. "Thanks for agreeing to do this, Marie," he breathed into her hair, and her skin prickled and flushed with the blood her haywire heart sent pounding.

She gave him a quick half hug back, but then stepped back.

"Let's go!" Agnes yelled. "Ready?" she asked and everyone responded with an empathic *yes*.

Van missed the stop mark the first time. Marie, to her complete embarrassment missed it nine times after that. Marie thought the first few efforts sounded clumsy, Van was reciting his lines like the Tin Man, and she was overcompensating and sounded like a cheerleader on speed.

"Van," she said, tugging on his arm after the

tenth take. "Let's not read the script," she suggested. "It's killing our chemistry."

Van looked horrified. "Off script?"

"Yeah, we know the gist of what we're supposed to say, so let's just wing it."

"Marie…" Van's eyebrows clashed in the middle of his forehead. "I don't wing it."

Somehow that did not surprise her. "Well, we have to do something, because right now we suck."

Van took a deep breath and started nodding his head. "Okay, okay I'll ah… I'll try to wing it."

One take later they were loosened up and trading verbal jabs along with some tips to finding the best Chinatown had to offer. From barbecued duck, to spices hand-ground by virgins, to snake, to herbs, and the strange delicacy—one-hundred-year-old egg.

The intro ended, like all the intros were scheduled to end. "Good food should be an adventure," Van said. And Marie looked into the black eye of the camera and said, "Come on, I dare you."

"And cut!" Agnes yelled. "Great job guys, let's move on."

Van looked a little shell-shocked, so Marie patted him on the arm. "You okay?" she asked. *I want to kiss him.* It could be the excitement of the show or the mascara he was wearing, whatever it was Marie was dying to kiss him.

"I am awesome!" he said and shrugged. "I am winging it."

You and me both, buddy, she thought.

The whole crew jumped back into the van and headed to her favorite place for hot-and-sour soup. She was fudging on the rules because it was Vietnamese soup, but so much of Chinatown was turning into noodle-and-soup houses that it made sense to highlight it in the show.

The name of the restaurant translated loosely into "good soup." The place was spare and empty as *AMSF* had reserved the small restaurant for an hour of shooting.

"Hello, Ling!" Marie waved to the proprietress who was waiting and ready behind her counter. Ling waved, bowed and beamed, and Marie felt great about being able to bring a little spotlight Ling's way.

Agnes ran around screaming about sound and light levels, and Van and Marie sat in their booth drinking hot tea.

Everyone was so busy that it seemed like Van and Marie were cocooned against it all, just by being still. Marie made a point of never looking Van too long in the eye, and as they sat across from each other she made sure there was no accidental knee bumping or finger touching.

She was in control of this.

He reached for the teapot and she pushed it across the table at him. Perhaps a little too hard since the tea sloshed out on his hand, but at least there was no touching in the transaction.

"We're going to have to do all of this over again at Palace Garden?" Van asked, watching the guys set up lights.

"'Fraid so."

"I should have just picked this place as my favorite, too."

Marie laughed at the idea. Van had picked the exact opposite of Ling's modest little shop. Palace Garden was a hallmark in luxuriousness, fountains, an orchid garden, linen tablecloths and ivory chopsticks.

"Of course you would love Palace Garden. Have you ever gone slumming, Van?"

"I'm with you aren't I?"

"Hardy-har." Marie took a sip of her tea and sighed.

"So, ah…where'd they find the egg?" Van asked and Marie sobered. Hundred-year-old eggs were no laughing matter.

Marie had seen them being made when she was working in China. The chef she was working for wanted one of the strange delicacies for a patron and Marie was sent on the case. She had found a little old woman who took fresh duck eggs and cured them in a muddy mixture of salt water, pine ash and lime for one hundred days, not years. But it made little difference. They were still vile.

"Some place around the corner from Palace Garden."

"Have you ever had one?"

"No, but I smelled one once." The little Chinese woman had cracked open one of her jars and Marie could still gag just remembering the smell. "It's awful, Van. Really, really bad."

"Side bet on who throws up first?" he asked with mischief and challenge in his eyes, and Marie had to look away and take a deep breath. Those little smiles of his were potent.

"You're on." They shook hands quickly across the table.

Marie looked over her shoulder to see what was happening with setup because suddenly the silence between them became all too fraught with what they weren't saying.

"Marie?" She could tell just by the tone of his voice that he wanted to talk about the near kiss on Friday.

"Look, Van." She jumped in feet first. "I know what you're going to say." She had to look away from his sincere and tender gaze.

"You do?" He cocked his head.

"Sure, you ah…" Why was this so hard? She had let dozens of men down easy in the past. What was the holdup here? "I know that the other morning it seemed like…" She rolled her hand in the air, suddenly at a loss for words.

"We were about to go at it backstage?" Van supplied when she was silent. He leaned forward a little so his voice wouldn't carry to the crew. "Are those the words you're looking for?"

"Those will do," she breathed. Somehow, just as the words came out of his mouth, she knew she wasn't in control of this situation. She kept getting sidetracked by the idea of…well, of them going at it backstage. She was distracted by his hand on the teacup. The veins that stood out in his wrist. She could smell him from across the table and it was killing her.

"So, what about it?" he asked, still leaning towards her.

"We can't do it."

"Can't?" He laughed once, a snort of objection. "Speak for yourself, Marie."

"Okay, fine. I can't, Van. It's a bad business decision. We should continue the way we are."

"What is that, exactly?"

"Partners, and maybe sometimes—" she found it hard to make this concession "—friends."

Van threw his head back and howled with laughter. The crew and everyone turned to look at them.

"Shhhh." She tried to get him to be quiet before someone asked them what was so funny.

He cleared his throat. "You're telling me that you don't want to have sex with me because you're worried it will ruin the friendship?"

She nodded, emphatically.

"Marie." Something in his tone, a certain heat that wasn't there before, made her breath catch in her throat. "We're not that good of friends."

Marie's mouth fell open. People are supposed

to respect the "let's not screw up the friendship" line. It was foolproof and sacred. The holy cow of breaking up or putting off unattractive people. There was a reason it was a crowd favorite and it was because polite people don't say screw the friendship.

"Make jokes, Van. Fine."

"Who's joking? Marie, at this moment I want to sleep with you far more than I want to be your friend."

"Listen—"

"Are you going to try and tell me that you don't feel the same way?" He was right, but she would never ever admit it. "Okay, Marie. We can have it your way. We can just be friends if you can look me in the eye and tell me that you don't want me."

It was hard. Harder than she thought it would be, but in the end she got the job done. She looked him right in the eye and lied. "I don't want you."

Van continued to watch her and she forced herself not to look away. After a moment he reached out to touch her face. His fingers traced her cheek and she felt the touch in her belly and in her breasts, and to her complete dismay her lips parted on a small breath.

"You're lying," he breathed. His fingertip touched the corner of her mouth before his hand dropped back down to the table.

"All right guys, let's bring in the soup and get the last light reads," Agnes yelled.

Ling's daughters brought huge steaming bowls of soup and plates of cilantro, lime wedges and bean sprouts to add to the soup. They smiled and made shuffling bows but Marie didn't particularly notice.

She was too busy trying not to leap across the table and rip the clothes from Van's body.

10

"MARIE? WHERE DID all these people come from?" Jodi asked. Their usually well-orchestrated dance around the salad case and cash register was moving at triple speed due to the amazing lunch lineup out the door. Tuesdays were usually a good day but this was ridiculous!

"I have no idea," Marie breathed, grabbing to-go boxes from Jodi, bagging them and ringing up customers. "Pete, how you doing?"

"Fine," Pete mumbled and continued steaming milk and making espresso like a madman.

"How long can we keep this up?" Jodi asked, spooning wild-rice salad onto a plate. Some fell on the floor and she kicked it aside so no one would slip on it. Pete had slipped on a tomato slice earlier. He was fine, but there was no time for that kind of break in the action. Broken limbs, blood, anything could put an end to the very fragile hold they had on this afternoon rush. "How long is that line?"

Marie looked through the E in the Marie's Bistro that was painted on her window. "I can't see the end of it." She could, however, see that across the street there was a small group of people milling around outside of Sauvignon, which was very strange since his lunch crowd was not the strongest business of the day.

"Marie, we saw you on TV." Two of her regulars, Todd and Aaron, a gay couple who ran an antique store a few doors down, paid for their lentil salads and tuna-fish sandwiches. "You were great!" Aaron said.

"And hot," Todd added. "You two look fantastic."

Was this all because of the show? There was no way…was there?

"See!" A short balding man ordering Thai-beef salad to go turned to his friend. "I told you the camera adds ten pounds."

"What?" she asked, affronted a dozen different ways. These two were strangers and, while she didn't rely completely on repeat customers, newcomers discussing her weight never came in. Nor should they.

"Sorry," rude balding man's friend actually blushed and pushed up his glasses. "I saw you on TV this morning and convinced Matt to come in today. He didn't believe me when I said you looked like Jennifer Lopez. But in real life you don't so much. You're much prettier."

Marie's eyes nearly fell out of her head. The place was swarmed and she was being compared to Jennifer Lopez? She pushed her hand against the sharp end of the ticket spindle to see if this was a dream.

This *was* because of the show. The phone rang and Marie continued ringing people up as she answered.

"Hello?" She cradled the phone between her shoulder and ear.

"What the hell is going on, Marie?" It was Van and he was yelling and laughing over the noise in the background.

"I know," she yelled back. "Sorry," she whispered to the woman in front of the cash register.

"You've got a lineup!"

"So do you!" She felt like a kid with a great secret and the only other person who knew about it was Van.

In the background somebody on Van's end dropped something big and heavy and Marie winced.

"I gotta go!" he yelled. "I just wanted to say thanks. Thank you, Marie."

"No, Van thank—" But he had already hung up.

"Hey, gabby, in case you haven't noticed we're dying here," Jodi muttered. Marie hung up the phone and got back to the matter at hand. The rise of her cooking empire.

VAN WAVED ASIDE THE SMOKE from Mitch's cigar. The old man shook his head, and Van prepared himself for the worst. "You are making a terrible mistake. Terrible."

"Look, Mitch, it's not like I planned it."

"Are you sure?" He took his cigar out of his mouth, "Really sure?"

"Who plans these things?" Van asked. Van leaned down and pulled more weeds from Mitch's small garden. He had a little patch of land in a co-op organic garden a few blocks from his condo. Somehow he always managed to get Van to agree to help weed. It was a hell of a way to spend a Wednesday morning after apparently setting San Francisco on fire with *Adventures in Food*, but Van had things on his mind. Namely Marie. He poked at his feelings for Marie to see what was real, or maybe just a mirage created by their success and his very significant physical attraction to her, but what he felt seemed solid. "I didn't say that I am in love…."

"Good." Mitch smoked his cigar and contemplated the top-most tomatoes on his tomato plant. "Don't say it." He picked one tomato and placed it in the basket over his arm.

"So what do I do, Mitch?" He felt squashed between a rock and a hard place. "I am crazy about her. I can't stop thinking about her. I want her so bad my fingers twitch whenever she's close. I want to talk to her, I want to feed her and watch—"

"I get the idea." Mitch scowled.

These feelings he had for Marie came way out of left field. She was the opposite of what he would have dreamed for himself, but at the same time, he couldn't imagine being attracted to someone more perfect. He was attracted to her class and her wit and her independence, her looks didn't hurt, either. But he had come to realize over the past few weeks that there was so much more to Marie than her pretty face.

But she said no, even though her eyes screamed yes. And they were partners…sort of. Which was why he was pulling weeds and trying to get some advice.

"What have I told you a dozen times?" Mitch asked, moving on to his green beans.

"Not to mix business and pleasure."

"That's right." Mitch nodded and some of his wild white hair waved in the breeze. "A successful kitchen is not something you fool around with."

"We're not sharing a kitchen."

"No." Mitch poked his cigar at Van. "You are sharing something much more important. This is your career, your reputation and you are putting it up on television for the whole world to see."

"Well, San Francisco is big but it's—"

"It won't just be San Francisco. This show is going to be huge," said Mitch with the tone of someone who knew. "And if you do this, if you mess with this…" He shook his head again and bent back over his green beans, like it was just too much to deal with.

Van crouched by the basil plants, nearly overgrown with weeds. He understood Mitch's point. It was a bad idea to muddle this situation up with sex, but on the other hand, he truly had the feeling that if he let Marie go, he would be missing something spectacular.

What was the big deal anyway? They were adults. Most of the time. He couldn't stop thinking about her and he was beginning to lose it.

In his frustration, he accidentally pulled out a basil plant and tried to replant the fragile roots. "You married your *sous chef*, Mitch. Are you trying to tell me that you wish you hadn't done it?"

"No, absolutely not. But we paid a price for it."

Van gave up on the plant and stood up, dusting his hands off on his pants. "Everything costs something," he said and meant it. He had given up so much to be a chef, to have his own business, but the rewards were worth it.

And, he thought, *Marie might just be worth it.*

"I'm going to do it," he said definitively and he was suddenly able to take deep breaths and think clearly. This was the right thing to do. He was sure of it. Well, pretty sure. He was hovering at around sixty-five percent sure. "I'm going to try to woo Marie Simmons." He looked at Mitch, ready to take it on the chin from the old man, but Mitch was smiling around his cigar.

"This should be good," the old man said.

VAN DIDN'T QUITE KNOW how to go about seducing Marie. She definitely wasn't like other women. Flowers, wine, all of that seemed a bit trite for Marie. He needed to think bigger, better. But then

she took the problem right out of his hands and arrived at his kitchen door on Friday with the money
she owed him from their hundred year old egg bet.

"No one could ever call you a sore loser," Van
said, taking Marie's hundred bucks. He had been
as surprised as she was when she threw up. He
had told her that she didn't need to pay him; he
knew that she was as strapped for cash as he was,
but she had insisted.

"Fair is fair," she said stoically and Van smiled,
folding the money and putting it in the back
pocket of his black chef pants. It was strange having her in his kitchen; it was like she was seeing
him in his underwear or something.

"You want a tour?" he asked.

She shook the silver bracelets down her arm to
look at her watch and even the sound of that ha-
bitual gesture, something he had watched her do
a million times, had a certain power over him.
"Sure, I've got some time."

"Where did you get those bracelets?" he asked,
suddenly curious.

Marie looked down at her wrist, at the bracelets, like she hadn't seen them in a while. "Some
in Arizona. I got them when I was a kid. Some
other places."

"You're still a kid," he told her. "Totally a kid."

"Hardy-har, show me your palace, King Van."
They walked through his kitchen and that standing-
around-in-his-underwear feeling only got worse.

The exposed-brick oven for his legendary pizzas was a focal point next to his grill and stove. His copper pots hung from the ceiling in a sort of artistic jumble that always pleased him. He watched her out of the corner of his eye to see if it pleased her.

"I have a confession to make, Van," she said.

"I love a good confession," he joked.

"You were in a bidding war for this place weren't you?"

Ugh, just the memory of those tense days had enough power to bring back heartburn. "I was. How did you know?"

"I was the other bidder."

How incredibly fitting—even before he actually met her, she was making him crazy. "I should have let you have it," he told her.

"I hate to rub it in, but I'm glad you got saddled with the sewage."

"Thanks," he drawled and continued the tour, allowing himself to put his hand in the small of her back. Once. And just for a moment.

Van let her taste the sauces bubbling on his stove and was extraordinarily flattered when her eyes lit up and she declared his red sauce the best she had ever tasted. He talked about his home-made pasta and showed her the crabmeat ravioli that one of his line chefs was making.

She asked about his bread and he told her who made it. She shook her head, tsk-tsking like Mrs. Blakely in the sixth grade.

"What's wrong with Deuce Breads?" He leaned back against his stainless-steel counter and crossed his arms over his chest.

"Nothing if you're fond of sawdust…" She pinched the end of a slab of focaccia.

"You know a better baker?" he asked, liking this light teasing and the easy back and forth. But he was unprepared for the intensity of the smile she gave him and what it did to his stomach, the warmth it gave to his chest.

"Van, are you offering me a job?" She put a hand on his shoulder and he felt the jump of shocking static that her flesh passed to his body. He wished they could just kill this tension by having sex and getting it out in the open. Maybe then he could talk to her without staring at her breasts.

You're thirty-four, not fourteen, he reminded himself, but it did no good. She took a deep breath and he swallowed a groan.

"No, but I might be offering you a contract."

"One step at a time, Van. Show me your dining room."

Van nodded and led the way through the swinging doors into his badly painted, completely undecorated and dimly lit dining room. Standing at those doors, he felt like he had shucked the underwear and was now standing naked in front of her. On a cold day.

The lights were off but the sunlight slanting

through the front windows made the walls look like they were covered in Pepto-Bismol.

"Good God, your walls are pink!" Marie exclaimed, looking horrified and delighted at the same time. "Van. Your walls..."

"I know, I know," he said, waving her off. "I keep the lights low so it looks red."

She laughed, great peals of laughter that she tried to quell when she caught his face. "I'm sorry, but you...oh, God. Mr. Man has pink walls. It's perfect."

"Are you done?"

She tried to keep her face straight. "Yes."

"You're biting your lips!"

She nodded, her eyes closed.

"You're still laughing."

She took a deep breath, looked at the walls and lost it again. "Rough, ready and masculine has got hot-pink walls. I love it!" she squealed and actually clapped her hands.

Van walked to the bar and poured himself a cup of coffee while she got herself together.

"Van, the room is gorgeous." She looked around, slowly turning and Van got the sudden feeling that she might just be the brightest thing in his life. The one thing that glowed with its own power. "Look at all the wood. Mahogany wainscoting and the dark high booths. It's gorgeous. Those old milk glass lights and this bar..." She walked up to the bar and slid her hands across the polished cherrywood.

"Where'd you get it?" she asked as her bracelets slid across the wood, jangling musically.

"Mexico." He took a sip of his coffee, watching her hands and the bracelets over the edge of his cup. "What is the deal with the bracelets?"

Marie touched them. Van counted five bracelets on each wrist.

"Are they for your secret children?"

Marie laughed and Van leaned down over the counter, so their elbows and shoulders almost touched. He swayed a bit just to measure the distance.

"No secret children."

"Ex-husbands?"

"Definitely not," she laughed, but he knew her well enough to know that it wasn't real. It lacked the usual music and magic.

She continued to touch the small silver bangles, and because they were alone and it was quiet and still in his restaurant, he reached over and touched the tip of his finger to one of the bracelets. It was warm from her skin and his body tensed with the realization.

"Five mistakes," she breathed. "Five lessons." She tossed her hair over her shoulder and he caught the smell of her.

"You want to tell me about them?"

They stared at each other for so long that Van almost took the invitation that was always between them. He almost leaned in to press his lips to hers, to see if her skin tasted like it smelled, was as soft as it looked.

"Later, perhaps." She pushed away from the bar and Van had to smile. He hadn't been this wound up about a girl since he was fourteen. "Back to work for me."

She went to his front door, the sunlight making a halo around her dark body as she walked through his restaurant. He was reminded of an eclipse, the small perfect body of the moon passing in front of the sun.

"Marie…" She turned, her hair settling over her shoulder. "Someday it's going to happen between us." He braced his arms against the bar and watched her. "You know that, right? It's inevitable."

She smiled, the coy, knowing smile that made him nuts. "We'll see, Van. We'll see."

The door opened, the noise of outside leaked in, horns and cars and people shouting, and Marie stepped out onto the sidewalk. He saw her look left, holding up her hand to shade her eyes from the bright sun that had come out the last few days. Then the door closed and he was left alone again in the scent of basil and lemon that lingered in the darkness of his restaurant.

11

"THAT'S A CRABBING BOAT." Van stopped on the old wooden pier leading down to the commercial crabbing boat that they were going on for the day. Marie, following Van, plowed into his back, still asleep in the very early morning. The urge to stay there, touching his warm back, maybe wrapping her arms around his long, lean waist and fall asleep in the…

Whoa there, hot to trot. She stepped away and felt the chilly wind seep in between the front of her warm jacket and the back of his.

It was very early Sunday morning and they were filming the crabbing segment for their second show. It had been two days since Van's bald statement of intent. *It's inevitable, Marie.* His words echoed all through her sleepless nights, following her as she rolled across her large empty bed, as she took a cold shower and had a shot of whiskey to try to take the sharp edges off her nerves and libido.

Finally, drunk, fed up and turned on, she touched herself for some relief, imagining the strength and breadth of Van's hands the entire time.

Marie peered around Van's shoulder at the

small diesel crabbing boat with the round cages stacked up at the back like tires. The old putt-putt floated at the end of the dock like a relic. A seaworthy memory of what the San Francisco harbor used to look like. The hull might have once been green, but now was sort of gray with dreams of being green toward the top, by the deck.

The crew in the bright orange slickers was waiting for them. She lifted her hand in a wave and the crew waved back.

"There's been a mistake." Van whirled around, shaking his head.

"We're going crabbing, Van. That's a crab boat." Marie blinked at him.

"Yeah, I'm a chef doing a TV show going crabbing on a charter boat. Charter boat," he repeated a little more slowly, as if Marie were unfamiliar with the concept or words. "Charter boat as in heated cabin and comfortable chairs and someone else does all the work."

Marie lifted a shoulder. "Well, you're wrong. You're a chef on a TV show going crabbing on a commercial boat. Commercial. As in you better wear a life jacket and hope you don't fall overboard." She walked by him, breathing hot air on her cold and chapped hands. "Jeez, it's cold."

"People die on those boats, Marie,' Van whispered, falling in step right beside her. "They get their hands or feet caught in those ropes and they just get dragged overboard."

Marie was ignoring Van because he was the eternal pessimist and she wasn't going to let him bring her down.

Marie was excited about the crabbing segment.

She took a deep breath of the cold, salty air. The sun barely registered as a soft pink haze in the eastern sky. The western sky was still black as night.

I'd give my arm for a coffee, she thought.

"Marie," Van whispered as they were getting within hearing distance of the boat. "I'm serious."

I'd give Van for a cup of coffee.

"Hello, boys." She smiled at the crew of strong men, seemingly of Italian descent. "You giving us a ride?"

"You bet!" one of them answered and held out his hand for Marie to grab, but she quickly found her hand in Van's grasp.

"Excuse us a moment," he told the men and whirled her around to face the other direction. "Marie, this is not what I signed on for."

"It is, too. We are going crabbing. You signed on for crabbing."

Van looked heavenward, something he did when he most wanted to throttle her. She smiled. "Relax, Van." She even patted him on the shoulder and, because it was early and she was tired and he looked so cute wearing his dark blue stocking cap, she ran her hand down his arm.

His eyes narrowed. "Nice try. I'm still not getting on that boat."

"Sorry, Van." It was Agnes, the voice of authority, who joined Marie's side. "You're going to have to get on that boat." Agnes and her camera guy were walking down the pier toward them, wearing rain slickers and warm hats.

And carrying coffee. *Thank you, Lord.* Agnes handed a cup to Marie.

"Thought you might need this," Agnes said with a sharp smile.

"I would marry you, Agnes, I really would," Marie said, taking the cup from the producer. She noticed that with Agnes and her camera guy there was another man she hadn't seen before. Small and blond and just as miserable-looking as the rest of them. She was about to ask Agnes about him, but Van cut in.

"Agnes, I get that this is supposed to be about adventure, but these things can be really dangerous." Van was unreasonably trying to be reasonable, and perhaps it was misplaced joy over the coffee, but Marie just thought he was adorable.

"Don't be a baby, Van. It's a boat, it's fishing. These guys aren't going to kill us. That's bad press."

Agnes and the camera crew nodded in agreement.

"Hey! Can we get this show on the road or what?" one of the guys, perhaps the captain, yelled from the boat, and Agnes, Mike, the cameraman and Marie all looked at Van.

"If I die—" he shook his finger at Marie "—I'm haunting you for the rest of your life. You'll never sleep again."

Yeah, and what else is new? she thought.

Agnes and Mike headed over to the boat and Marie and Van followed a little behind. "Ah, Marie…" Van started.

"Yes, baby?"

"Don't. I'm being serious." Van was whispering and Marie looked at him as they walked. "Marie." He stopped and she stopped as well, puzzled by his meek behavior.

"Van?"

"I can't swim."

ONCE THE SUN CAME UP and they were out on the water, Van gave a little spiel about the Dungeness crab while wearing a life jacket and a harness that firmly attached him to the boat. He looked ridiculous and Marie, standing beside him without a life jacket, made sure that the television audience knew it.

"The Dungeness crab—"

"Would you feel better if you had some water wings?" Marie asked, twirling the end of her harness in what she hoped was a devil-may-care fashion. "We should have brought you a lifeguard."

"I'd feel better if we could drop you down in these crab pots," he said without looking at her. The crew of the boat and Mike, the cameraman, snorted.

They talked about the pots and what kind of bait the crab men were going to use in the bait jars. As time went on, Van got more and more comfortable, and actually walked around the ship, stepping rather shakily across the slick deck, only grabbing on to something solid as they rode the downward slope of the waves.

Marie went to help the crew of the boat lower the cages into the water. As she bent over the side, the old boat met a wave head on and Marie got a face full of seawater.

"Did you get that on tape?" Van asked, laughing his stupid head off. Marie swiped wet hair from her eyes and glared at Van, who only shrugged.

"This was your idea, Marie."

"This was your idea, Marie," she mocked like a fourth grader as she turned around to grab the next pot. "Why aren't you helping, Van?" she shouted.

"I am. Someone has to tell the viewing audience how funny it is when you get pelted in the face with a wave."

She scowled at him over her shoulder, but he was unmoved by the bad vibes she was throwing his way.

Soon, the sun was all the way up, though it was still cold and Marie's shirt underneath her slicker was almost soaked with the errant waves that had battered her during the early morning. Her hair was wet and cold, her lips were chapped and she'd cut her hand on one of the cages.

Crabbing was stupid. She hated crabbing.

After they had baited all the cages and thrown or kicked them into the water, it was time to go and pick up the cages the men had baited and thrown yesterday.

Van finally decided to get to work pulling up the cages filled with crabs, which Marie did recognize as being much harder than kicking the empty cages into the water. But Van didn't get smashed in the face by a wave once. And he looked pretty hot working hard out on the water.

He and one of the crew members were pulling up the ropes, their arms straining against their shirts. Van had rolled up his sleeves, and the muscles and tendons in his forearms pulsed with the effort. Marie, cold and miserable, felt a little warmer as she watched him. He was beautiful in the clear and bright sunlight. He practically glittered. They finally got the cage up, filled with snapping, angry crabs and Van laughed, wiping the sweat off his forehead.

"I think I pulled every muscle in my body," he said, hamming it up for the camera. Marie smiled, though her mind was occupied by other things. Like Van. And her sincere hope that she had been wrong about the small penis. Because she was going to find out.

"THAT WAS PRETTY FUN, I've got to say...." Van said. He had picked her up at dawn this morning and was now returning her home, damp and frustrated.

"It was supposed to be fun for me," Marie insisted, "and awful for you. That was the point."

"Who's being the baby now, huh?" He wiggled his out-of-control eyebrows at her and Marie fought the urge to stick out her tongue.

The day out on the ocean had put red in his cheeks and a certain glint in his eye.

Started off the dumb guy couldn't swim, now he's Ahab. She thought bitterly and was ashamed of herself. It was no fun being the comic relief side kick when you wanted to be the heroic lead. Who didn't get sea sick.

Van parked his car on the side street of her restaurant and apartment. He pulled the parking brake and waggled the gear shift. Marie was out the door and heading for dry clothes before Van could even get his keys out of the ignition.

"Come on up," she shouted over her shoulder, knowing she was inviting the devil into her house. But she didn't care. "We'll have some tea."

Van climbed the shaky wooden steps to Marie's apartment. He pulled out the keys she had left in the lock of her purple door and stepped into her home. He felt like there might be land mines, someplace, just waiting for him.

Van imagined his picture skewered to a dartboard. At the very least there was going to be something black and lacy on the floor or hung over a doorknob.

He hoped so.

Instead of underwear there were dozens of tea-cups and mugs littering the floor surrounding every possible place there was to sit. Magazines and papers, half-eaten… Van leaned down to try to identify the mysterious object left on a plate. He poked it. It didn't poke back and Van guessed it was a croissant.

"Whoa," he breathed, looking around. "She is a slob."

A slob yes, but a slob with impeccable taste. Past the crap strewn everywhere, he could see the charm that made Marie's Bistro so appealing to the entire city.

Her living room was a faint green color like the white sage that grew up in the mountains and her house even sort of smelled like sage. One entire wall was a bookshelf, filled with art and food books. He recognized the well-worn spines of Mitch's books and his respect for Marie went up another notch.

"Sorry the place is such a mess," Marie walked into the room and leaned against the door frame. "Housekeeping is way low on my list of priorities." She brushed her damp hair, her arms lifted behind her head as she worked out tangles. Her breasts pressed in fantastic relief against an old AC/DC concert T-shirt.

Think calming thoughts, think calming thoughts, Van told himself, looking up at the ceiling to regain his equilibrium.

Van noticed she wasn't hurrying around trying to tidy her place up. He liked that about her; she was always unapologetically herself.

"Come on into the kitchen. Mint tea all right?" She turned and walked out of the living room and he followed her into the kitchen, which was orange and warm with wooden countertops and open shelves that displayed jars of spices, rice, pasta and beans.

"Mint tea's fine." He was taking in every aspect of her home. This house seemed deeply personal and just the fact that he was here, in her orange kitchen about to drink tea from earthenware mugs made him feel closer to her. She had taken off the invisible armor that always surrounded her and Van knew he was seeing the real Marie.

She had changed into a pair of jeans with a patch on the butt that Van found riveting. He tried to look away and noticed she had bare feet, which were lovely, but they had nothing on that little patch on her ass.

Something's got to happen, he thought, breathing hard and trying to divert the blood from his groin.

She poured hot water into their mugs and started to hum, horribly off-key. She tilted her head, the sun coming in the window filtered through her damp black curls, turning them red at the tips, and Van felt something clench in his chest. Something impossible and almost painful.

"Did Agnes tell you who that guy was on the

dock this morning?" she asked, looking over her shoulder at him. Van was immediately pulled out of his reverie about getting Marie naked.

"No," he answered. He took the mug from her and she leaned back against the opposite counter, the window and the dim sunshine behind her. "What guy?"

"He didn't come on the boat with us but he was there on the dock with Agnes and the crew."

"Probably just a new crew member." Van shrugged. He had been far too occupied with freaking out to notice a strange man.

"Yeah," she nodded. "You're probably right." But it was clear she didn't believe either of them.

"I guess I'll just give myself a tour?" he asked.

"There's not much to see," she told him. "If you stand at the kitchen sink you can see into every room.

"You should see my condo. If you stand by the kitchen sink you're just about standing in every room." Van was trying so hard to play it cool, but in reality he was starving to find out more about this woman he was growing obsessed with.

To his left Marie had a long hallway painted red that he presumed led back to her bedroom. *Whatever you do, don't think about the bedroom.*

The hallway walls were covered in photos. Van walked to examine them, his hands in his pockets, the very picture of a casual friend, but he was absorbing every detail he could find that would tell him more about Marie.

He recognized the major places in the photos, the Eiffel Tower, a couple of cathedrals, lots of mountains, that place in Peru that sounded like the name of a dog. Photos of a hundred far off places and most of them were just landscapes. There were a few photos of a woman that had to be Marie's sister, with long straight black hair rather than Marie's gypsy curls. There were some men, one man in particular in most of the shots from France.

Marie was in a couple, young and obviously headstrong, still working out her fashion sense. He shook his head, reached up to straighten a photo of Marie and a young man in front of the rolling hills of a vineyard.

"What?" she asked, her voice quiet in the hush of her apartment. She stood at his elbow and it took all his strength not to curl his arm around her shoulder and pull her close.

"You look like trouble." He pointed to a picture of her in London's Piccadilly Circus. She was wearing leather and a scowl.

"I was." She put on the scowl again, making fun of herself and that was it. End of the line. She was close enough to touch, and so he did.

He cupped her cheek, slid his palm back so his fingers touched her hair and his thumb rested at the corner of her mouth. And her skin was just what he thought it would be, soft and silky and warm. "Why aren't we making love, Marie?"

"I think we're about to," she breathed. *Oh my God*, he thought, suddenly a fourteen-year-old boy again.

"Have you decided to trust me, then?"

"No," she smiled. "I've just decided to have sex with you." Van had a strange instinct to say *that's not enough for me*, but he squelched it in time. He couldn't believe it, could barely understand the changes that were suddenly happening in him.

Her hands came up to his waist and it was enough to make him catch his breath. "Kiss me, Van. Let's get this over with." Her words were flip, but her eyes were hot and serious with an intensity he had never seen in her. His blood beat hard through veins that were suddenly too small, through skin that was suddenly too tight. Van realized with a sort of thrill that he had never felt this way.

He leaned in, drawing the moment out as much as he could. This was it, his first kiss with Marie Simmons, and he wanted it to last. He wanted to savor it, take his time, roll her over his tongue and memorize the taste of her.

She laughed, grabbed his head and kissed him with her smiling gypsy mouth.

His hand clenched reflexively in her hair and she gasped against his lips and the joking ended. She leaned up against him, those full breasts finally...*oh, thank you*...pressed against him. He cupped her head, lifting her taller, and when he opened his mouth, hers was already open. His tongue touched hers, tasted her, mint tea and toothpaste. She licked his lips and they fell back against the wall.

Her body was a warm curve against him, pressed hard against the wall. He could feel her nipples, the rise of her pubis against his thigh and he saw stars behind his closed eyelids.

She pressed harder against him, turned her head to get closer.

"Marie," he panted into her mouth.

Her hands slid down to his ass, grabbing him for leverage as she lifted harder, higher against him. He pressed his palm against her hip, felt that patch against his fingers and flexed his hands, loving the firmness of her, the lushness of Marie. He hiked her up higher, suddenly on fire to get the centers of their bodies to touch, even if it was through denim.

"Yes," she hissed throwing out her arm for balance. She knocked a photo off the wall. It thumped against the floor and fell over on its face.

"Mar—"

"I don't care," she breathed into his mouth. "I don't care."

Well, he certainly didn't, either.

It was feverish between them. Insane. Her hands were everywhere. He felt as if they were sliding and before he knew it, his knees hit the floor. She slipped sideways, sucking his tongue, pressing her fingertips under the waistband of his pants and he followed her until they were lying on the floor of Marie's hallway.

In the back of his head he thought maybe he should bring up the bed that had to be around here somewhere, but in the end it didn't matter. Nothing mattered but Marie and the wild things going on in his body.

He lifted his hand from the patch on her pants to just under the hem of her T-shirt. She arched into his hand, pushing his own shirt up and he finally found the promised land underneath Angus Young on the front of her shirt.

He groaned, "Marie, you're amazing." Her breasts were round and warm and full underneath the lace of her bra. His thumb found her nipple and he scraped it slightly and she groaned again.

"So are you," Marie whispered, her hands on his chest. Van tried not think about how long it had been since his body had seen a gym.

He pulled his mouth away from Marie's and bent to her breasts. He carefully bit, through the T-shirt, her nipples, pushing them higher. He slid her shirt up to her neck and she did the rest of the work, wrenching Angus over her head. Her breasts were spilling out of the white lace cups of her bra and he did the best he could to convey to

Marie his heartfelt appreciation of her breasts with his mouth and his fingers. From the way she writhed and her breath hitched, Van guessed she got the picture.

At some point his own shirt came off and her mouth was on his chest, her tongue tracing its way across his neck, to his ear, down the bare skin of his chest.

"Marie," he gasped, "you're killing me."

They pulled back, looking at each other, and her smile sent rockets off in his head.

"Good," she told him. "You've been killing me for months."

He kissed her again, softly, gently, trying somehow to tell her the impossible way he felt without actually telling her. He didn't know a lot but he guessed telling Marie that he might be in love with her would be a mistake. So he made love to her mouth and with a slow and sure hand, he undid the button on her pants.

He slid his hand across the soft warm skin of her stomach and fell immediately in love with that part of her. He tore his mouth from hers and brushed kisses down her breasts, previously his favorite body part until he got to her completely enchanting belly.

She pushed on his head, trying to convince him to move on, but he was prone to linger at her belly button. She had an outie. It was adorable. All of her was adorable. He brushed his cheeks against the skin of her stomach wondering if he had ever felt anything so soft.

"Van…?"

"You have a perfect belly button."

"Thank you," she laughed. "But how about we move this along…"

"Sure." He kissed her there at the small knot of flesh, she moaned, throwing one arm over her eyes. "But it's just so perfect."

Marie pushed on his shoulders and he rolled over onto his back. Marie straddled him, her black hair wild around her face, curling around her breasts. She yanked at his belt, sliding it through the loops and then tossing it over her shoulder with a wicked grin.

He rubbed his hands up the taut strong muscles of her legs. *She's got great legs*, he thought, wondering how many of her body parts he could worship and if he could do it for the next several days or years, maybe. "You're killing our pace, Van."

"It looks like you're ready to make up some time."

She nodded and unzipped his pants. She bit her lip as her hand eased into the waistband of his boxers. He held his breath against the urge to sing the hallelujah chorus, but she seemed slightly apprehensive.

"Phew," she breathed as her hand measured the length of his penis. He was no slouch, but that was certainly a first.

"What?" he gasped, panting for air as she continued stroking him.

She leaned down, kissed him hard on the lips and started pulling off his pants. "I'll tell you later."

12

THREE HOURS LATER Marie was trying hard to get out of her own bed, but Van had a firm grip on her hand and, honestly, she didn't want to leave. But the restaurant could be burning down. Well, probably not, but she knew there were no afternoon baguettes to go out because she hadn't baked them and someone had to make the dairy order. Duty called, though Van's bare chest and the look in his eye were making some noise of their own.

"You thought I had a tiny penis?"

"No," she corrected, slipping her legs over the side of the bed. "I hoped you had a small penis." She stood up and he yanked her back down and she bounced on the mattress. "I thought you deserved a small penis," she laughed as he leaned over her.

"I don't think that's funny, Marie."

"Well, we're both relieved that I was wrong." She stroked his face and leaned up to kiss his full warm lips.

Her heart felt huge, too big for the small confines of her body. Part of it she knew was the sex; amazing sex was one hell of a mood lifter. But the other part of it was Van.

He makes me feel good, she thought and the realization made her nervous.

"Van, I really have to go and make sure everything is fine."

"Okay." Van pulled away. "But come back. My penis and I have some things we want to say to you." He reclined against her red sheets, his arms behind his head, and Marie's breath caught in her throat.

Marie threw on some clothes and raced downstairs. She yanked open the back door into the kitchen and was arrested by the smell of baking bread.

Pete was cleaning up flour from the wooden countertop that was used for rolling out dough. Pete, himself, was covered in flour.

"Hey Marie!" Jodi came waltzing in from the front, grinning. "Your shirt's on backwards."

"What's going on?" she asked. To her complete astonishment, Jodi walked up to Pete and started patting some of the flour from his shirt and pants. *She's touching his butt!* As far as Marie knew these two had never even spoken to each other in her presence.

Neither said anything; Pete's blush beneath the dreadlocks and the flour on his face were enough.

Marie belatedly put two and two together.

"Pete?" Marie asked, flabbergasted. "Your mystery guy is Pete?"

"Yep," Jodi nodded and looked fondly at the man who clearly wished he was anywhere else but here. Marie laughed and clapped her hands. *Great. Love and sex and happiness for everyone.*

"I can't believe it, but good for you guys."

"Yeah, it kind of surprised us, too," Jodi said.

The timer went off on the oven and Marie was reminded that her silent barista who was in love with the assistant manager was also, it seemed, a baker.

Pete opened the oven and sprayed the oven walls with water so the bread crust would be chewy. Marie looked into the oven and the baguettes looked gorgeous. They were still soft and white but turning brown on top. Had she done the baguettes, they would not have looked better. "How did you learn to do all of this?" she asked Pete.

"I watched you," he said, shrugging. He shut the oven door.

"He's been reading about bread and cooking since he started working here," Jodi piped in. "He wants to be a baker."

Marie took a step backward and leaned up against the kitchen door. "You're joking."

Pete shook his head. "I like it."

"Yeah, but would you like it at 3:00 a.m.?" she

asked. The answer to her baker problems was Pete? Amazing. "Because that's when ninety percent of the baking is done."

"Sure." He glanced at Jodi who was beaming. She nodded her head, encouraging him, and Pete's face changed. He stood a little straighter, shook his hair out of his eyes and turned back to Marie a different guy. "Marie, I would like to stop making coffee and be a baker, and maybe a cook even," he told her. They were the most words she had ever heard him say.

"Done." Marie grabbed Pete by the shoulders and hugged him. "Done. Wednesday morning, 3:00 a.m. Baking 101." She grabbed Jodi and hugged her. "You jerk, keeping all these secrets."

Jodi pulled back and carefully looked over Marie's face. "I think you've got some of your own secrets," she whispered.

Marie thought of the pirate chef in her bed. "I'll be back in an hour, guys." Marie took off running for the back stairs.

"So, Sam has finally given up his dream of naming the baby after his grandfather. Otto is not a name a kid needs to be saddled with." Anna was on a roll. It was Monday, Marie's day off and Marie had thought a walk through Golden Gate Park would do her and her sister some good. It would also give her a chance to spill her guts about Van and the last week. But so far Anna had been having her own little soliloquy, and not that Marie wasn't completely riveted by Sam's ancestral names, but she had news! News of the best kind.

"He also likes Jesse but I'm more inclined…"

"I had sex with Van."

Anna stopped dead in her tracks, her mouth agape. *Well, that shut her up.* "When?" Anna breathed, her eyes slowly beginning to twinkle.

"A week ago."

"A week ago!" she shrieked. "And I am just hearing about this?"

"Shhhh, let's walk and talk and try not to alert everyone of my love life," Marie muttered, pulling her sister back into motion.

"You had sex?" she whispered, scandalized. "With Van?"

"I did." *I did,* she thought, feeling loose and languid in places that had previously been tight and neglected.

"Details! Dirty ones." Anna hopped up and down and Marie looked at her askance. Anna liked the occasional full disclosure sex conversation as much as any other woman, but Marie had never seen Anna quite so desperate before.

"You really are hard up, aren't you?"

"You have no idea," Anna said and they continued their stroll.

"Do I need to have a conversation with Sam about leaving my sister unsatisfied?"

Anna shook her head and started to blush,

which was a good sign of something juicy. "Oh, who's got news to spill now?" Marie asked.

"Marie, it's not that I am not having sex, it's that I am not having enough sex."

"So, tell him…"

"Marie, there's only so much one man can do," Anna whispered. Marie stopped walking and looked at her reserved sister with newfound respect. "It's the hormones, they're making me crazy! Come on, don't look like that. Keep walking. And we're talking about you and your sex life."

"Well that's pretty much all I've got. I had sex with Van." She was lying. Sex didn't begin to describe what had happened on her hallway floor. There was sex as she had known it and then there was Van on the hallway floor. Worlds apart.

"Where?"

"Hallway floor. Shower. Rocking chair."

"Rocking chair?"

Marie shrugged feeling flushed and womanly. "The man's got skills."

"Nice."

"Thank you."

Anna slid her arm through Marie's and they walked in comfortable silence for a while. An old woman who had to be ninety if she was a day passed them in a motorized wheelchair. "So what's that mean for the two of you?"

Marie exhaled through her nose, knowing that question was coming. "I don't know." It was the truth and it was the last thing she wanted to get into for a million murky reasons. Dark pools from the past that she didn't want to dip her toe into. But she knew that Van was not a casual man. Everything about him, from his restaurant to his car to his devotion to Mitch screamed that he was a guy who held on. And when he kissed her belly and watched her when he thought she was sleeping, tucking her hair behind her ears and breathing kisses against her shoulder, she knew that he wasn't casual about her. And that scared her. Scared the crap out of her.

She had been hurt so much in the past. Burned to the bone and she didn't know if she had it in her to try again.

When your mother kicks you out of the house at age sixteen and your fiancé abandons you for greener pastures, trust isn't something you hand out to people like a business card. The little bit she had left was locked up tight. And she didn't have the slightest idea if she knew how to get it out. Or maybe this was a moot point, maybe this would all fall apart before she even needed to worry.

"I am a firm believer in if it seems too good to be true it probably is." Perhaps it was the sunshine or the recent sex and the resulting endorphins, but her credo sounded jaded to her own ears.

Anna looked at her, startled. "You sound like a bitter old woman."

"I sound like a realist."

"Remember when you made me promise to keep an open mind about Sam?" Anna asked, reminding Marie about the early days of Anna's relationship.

"I do. Best promise you ever made."

"Well, how about you promise the same thing?"

Marie laughed. "It's hardly the same thing. Anna, you were going to try and pass Sam off as a fake boyfriend."

Anna turned, her blue eyes flashing and Marie got her first undistracted look at what her sister was wearing. Anna, never what one could consider a fashion plate, was wearing a red long-sleeved shirt and maroon sweatpants. She looked like a big pregnant blood blister.

"What do you think about when you get dressed in the morning?" Marie asked Anna, tugging her back into motion.

"Don't change the subject. Promise you'll keep an open mind about Van. You act like it's a forgone conclusion that it's going to end."

"Everything ends—"

"Marie!" Anna yelled, losing her patience. "Just promise."

"Fine. I promise." Anything to keep her pregnant sister's head from spinning around, but in her mind Marie's fingers were crossed.

"Good," Anna winced a little and rubbed at her back. "I need to sit," she said and Marie pointed at a nearby park bench. Anna eased herself onto the wooden seat and picked up a newspaper someone had left there. "Uh-oh," she said. She folded the paper and lifted it to have a better look. "Have you seen this?" Anna's eyes were wide with laughter. "'The Van and Marie Watch,' it's in the Life section of the Sunday paper."

"What?" Marie reached over to tilt the paper so she could see it. Right there on the front page of the Life section was the TV columnist. Marie quickly scanned the column catching the words *hilarious, chemistry interesting* and *you haven't seen local television like this.*

Anna laughed and patted her sister on the head. "My little sister is famous."

Marie continued glancing through the article that seemed to rave about the show. There were pictures of her and Van, separate press photos and even their high-school senior photos. She winced at Van's picture. Those eyebrows were a serious burden for a sixteen-year-old. It looked like a cat was sitting on his face.

"I'm hungry. Let's get a cheeseburger. A bacon one."

Since Anna's hunger was a common refrain, Marie knew she could ignore it for a little while. Like the gas light in her VW, it wasn't serious until things started shaking.

A slow, satisfied smile spread across Marie's face. *Well, well,* she thought. She and Van were a very good team, in a couple of areas. Maybe they could do this. Business and love. She was older, wiser than she had been two years ago. Van definitely wasn't Ian. Perhaps they had a chance.

"Feed me," Anna demanded. Marie groaned and helped Anna to her feet. "Can we go to Sauvignon?"

"Sure," Marie answered as they walked back toward Marie's car. She wanted to see him. She wanted to touch him and watch him smile at her.

I'm in trouble, she thought. And the scariest part was she didn't seem to mind.

"VAN, THEY LOOK GREAT," she said, leaning over him in his bed later that night.

"I feel naked." They both ran their fingers across the fresh pink skin Marie had revealed when she convinced him to let her just "clean up" his eyebrows. A cleanup effort akin to the aftermath of the Exxon Valdez nightmare. It had taken some cajoling and the promise of various sex acts, but he finally succumbed, and her very handsome man was now devastating.

My man, she thought, thrilled and feeling silly. *Van's my man.* The reckless throwing around of her heart always made her giddy.

She ran her finger across the small ridge under his lip. "How'd you get this scar?" She touched his lips, pressing the edges together, making him pout. She pushed her leg under his, beneath blue blankets that did not match his black quilt or the strange burgundy color on his walls. He really was color-blind.

"Knife fight in the Sudan."

Marie laughed, "Be serious." He rolled her back into his pillows, pressing his face into her neck.

"Serious," he said into the skin of her shoulder. He kissed her there and she exhaled on a gasp. "I was fishing," he mumbled, kissing along the tendons of her neck until he reached her ear. He licked her earlobe and she shied away, giggling at the tickle. "I got my own hook caught in my own face."

Marie howled and Van pushed himself up on his elbow. "You tell anyone and I'll have to kill you."

"Sure." Marie rolled her eyes. "One thing I've noticed about you, Van, you're all bark, no bite."

He wrapped his fingers beneath the bracelets she wore on the right wrist, running the pads of his fingers across the inscriptions and designs that some of the silver bangles had. "Secret for a secret, Marie. Tell me about the bracelets."

Marie immediately tensed, feeling the ugly past crowding her. She could put him off, distract him. She could pretend that he hadn't asked, protect herself now from any future hurt that might come her way. Even though she had the feeling it was too late to board up the windows. Hurricane Van was already here.

"I'll tell you about one, since you only told me one of your secrets."

"I let you pluck my freaking eyebrows, Marie," he muttered as he studied each of her bracelets. Finally, he leaned down and kissed her newest bangle. The one with the least scratches and dings. "This one."

"Ah, wise choice, Van. The newest addition." She pushed herself up on her pillows so that her breasts were even with Van's eyes. He grinned lasciviously at her and she pulled up the sheet to her armpits.

"I got this bracelet from a man in Paris who sold jewelry underneath the Eiffel Tower."

"When?"

"Two years ago." She stalled here and looked up at Van, loving the fall of his dark hair over his forehead. *This is trust,* she thought, stroking his hair, *if I do this I can't go back.*

"Marie," he breathed, kissing her chin, her cheek and finally her lips. "Tell me."

Marie was putty in his hands.

"Okay," she laughed and Van slid back down to her side, but he held her very close and that pleased a basic part of her. "I had been living in Paris for a few months when I got a job as an apprentice baker."

"That must have been wonderful," Van mumbled, his fingers tracing her collarbone.

"Don't interrupt or I won't tell the story," she admonished playfully. It was enough that she was telling him the damn story, she didn't have to play around while they did it. Van nodded and was quiet, though his finger continued its lazy figure eight on her collarbone.

"I was at the bakery for three months before I met Ian who was the night manager for a nightclub across the street." Marie pulled the edge of the sheet between her fingers, pulling it taut and then letting it drop and pulling it taut again. "He would come into the bakery for lunch before going to work and he would flirt and we would talk. He seemed like a nice man." She swallowed. "Very handsome and I ah...I began to like him. We became lovers and I convinced myself at some point that I loved him. He confided in me that he wanted to open a restaurant." She laughed bitterly remembering the moment in painful clarity.

"And I thought, how perfect, you want to open a restaurant and I like being a baker and chef. Clearly, we were meant to be together."

"You were young, Marie, that's all," Van sighed, trying to neutralize her sarcasm.

Young and stupid. "Anyway he quit his job and I supported us for a few months while he found people who would invest. He showed me the property that he was going to buy and we made huge plans. This was not going to be a small café. We were going to change the world, cuisine, Paris. Nothing was going to be the same." She tried to make a joke of it, laughing at what had been, on her part anyway, honest zeal. "He convinced me to get another job. He told me that he had gotten another job because the backers were reluctant because of the size of our project. It was a lot of money if it failed."

Van kissed her shoulder and kept his mouth there, his moist breath hot on her skin. "I asked him if I should meet the backers, but he said he had it under control. I got another job. I gave him most of my savings. We moved in together to save money."

"What happened with the backers?" Van asked against her shoulder, cutting right to the point. He blinked and his eyelash brushed her skin and her nipples hardened under the blue sheet.

"They wouldn't invest with such a young, untried female chef."

"What did Ian do?"

Marie held it all in for one second, one more second of keeping all of this to herself and then on a long sigh, she let go of it.

"He found another chef and dumped me."

"No," Van breathed. He shook his head, his fingers stroking the side of her face.

"Yeah," Marie laughed and looked back down at the sheet that was now twisted in her hands. "He told me not to take it personally. I told him I thought we were in love and he—" she took a deep breath "—he said it was just business. I bought the two bracelets as I was leaving."

"Two?"

Marie shook her left arm, the bracelets falling into place at her wrist. Van touched the bracelet on her left arm that was identical to the bracelet on her right. "One to remind me that I have to take care of myself because no one will do that for me. And the other is a reminder that love and business are an unfortunate combination."

There. Done. I said it. She waited to see what he would say. Time slowed down unbearably. Van brushed her hand, and the more silent he was, the more she wished that she had kept her mouth shut. The urge to say something, anything to kill this awful moment of expectation, was strong, but she forced herself to just be silent. She wondered if she could fake a stroke.

"Van—" she started.

"Not always," Van murmured at the same time.

"What did you say?" she asked and he shifted in the bed so his eyes were level with hers.

"Love and business is not always a bad combination." Like you and me, he didn't say, but might as well have. His eyes said it.

It was no declaration of love, which was fine by her. There was already enough emotional vulnerability in this bed. His eyebrows, her bracelets; it's a wonder no one was crying.

"Maybe you're right," she breathed. He pushed through all the unsaid things between them to kiss her lips. The past, Ian, France, it all disappeared. Van had the power to banish all her demons. For now, anyway.

13

VAN HAD TO ADMIT HE THOUGHT the *Adventures in Food* version of *Iron Chef* was going to be impossible. But thanks to Simon's fantastic producing and, of course, the teamwork between him and Marie, it went off spectacularly.

They cooked live during the Tuesday morning *AMSF*. He and Marie got their secret ingredient—sweet potato—at 8:00 a.m. and they had an hour to put together as many dishes using that ingredient as possible.

"You're just happy because you won," Marie whispered as they finally got backstage. She looked as exhausted as he felt. Little damp curls were stuck to her neck. He had no idea it would be so hard—it was sweet potato for crying out loud. Of course, those little red lights didn't help.

"I thought you had me with your poppy-seed-and-sweet-potato pie, Marie. Honest, I've never had anything so good."

"Well, sweet-potato ice cream was inspired," she said and he tried not to preen. It meant a lot to hear that from her. She looked down at her watch. "I gotta run, Van."

"Okay." It was somehow agreed that they wouldn't kiss each other at work, and right now he wished they never had that unspoken agreement because he was dying to feel her against his lips, pressed along his body. It was fun today and it was fun because of her. "I'll call you."

"Good," she said and before he could walk away, or before he really knew what hit him, she had leaned up on tiptoe and pressed a hard kiss to his mouth. "Good," she breathed and Van's stomach tightened.

She was gone in the next second.

"Well." Van whirled toward Simon's voice behind him. "It seems something is going on between my cohosts." Simon was smiling but Van still wished the producer hadn't seen that kiss.

"It's nothing," Van lied and Simon snorted, obviously not believing him. "Really—"

"Stop, stop, we're all adults." Simon waved his hands. "Besides, we've got bigger fish to fry. Come on up to my office."

Van was wary. He gestured behind him, toward the way Marie had gone. "Maybe we should wait for Marie."

Simon made a big show of sucking air through his teeth. "We actually are going to meet *about* Marie."

A secret meeting. Van flashed back to that negotiation session at Marie's Bistro. She would kill him. Absolutely kill him.

"Simon, I promised…"

"I know, no secret meetings?" Simon nodded. "She made me promise that stuff before, too. That's what we need to talk about. It's not evil. It's actually in her best interest."

Van had two schools of thought here. One, he could tell Simon to screw it, keeping both him and Marie out of the loop and allowing Simon way too much room behind both their backs. Or, he could go into this meeting, see what Simon had to say and let Marie know about it.

"I'm right behind you." Van followed Simon up to his office.

The blond guy that had been hanging around the set for the last three shows was sitting in one of the chairs in front of Simon's desk.

Van, in that moment, fully understood what a sinking feeling was. Whatever was going on, it was big and he wished Marie were with him.

"Van, I'd like you to meet Eric Maxwell." Van shook the small man's hand and immediately wanted to wash his own hands. There was a definite slime vibe about the guy.

"Van, it's good to meet you." Eric's smile was slick and his teeth were far too white. Van couldn't trust a guy with teeth that white. "I'm a producer for Food TV in charge of new programs."

Van's heart leaped and he hauled in a lungful

of air. This was huge. Bigger than he could have dreamed. He looked at Simon who was grinning like the Cheshire cat. "Wow."

"Yes, wow." Eric, commandeering Simon's office, gestured to the other hard wooden chair. "Have a seat, we want to talk to you about *Adventures in Food*."

Van sat. "You're interested?"

"Well," Eric Maxwell said, crossing his legs like a woman. Van really couldn't trust a guy who crossed his legs like a woman. "You've got some great things going for you. Chemistry, knowledge, and your looks don't hurt. But—" Eric made a strange wincing expression "—there's a problem."

"What?"

"We only want one of you. Cohosts, particularly male and female, don't work with our audiences."

Van's chin dropped to the floor. "You want me to bail on Marie?" He looked in outrage at Simon. *That bastard, how many times does he have to screw that woman out of…*

"Actually we want Marie," Eric cut in trying to look pained but he only looked slimier. "Sorry. Our industry has been without a Martha for too long. We need a guru of style and taste and Marie really is the right woman at the right time."

Van's pride reeled from the hit and his outrage woke up with a roar. "You want Marie to bail on me?"

"There is always a home here for you at *AMSF*,"

Simon butted in. "And Marie's show wouldn't start until your contract ended."

"*Adventures in Food* is so popular. Simon, why the hell are you doing this?" Van stood up, his chair screeching across the floor. He couldn't believe it, after all the hard work he had put into this, that all of them had put into *Adventures in Food*, they wanted to split it up. "You're our producer."

Simon's ears turned red.

"He's done amazing work with *Adventures in Food* and we've offered him a job." Eric stood as well.

"Of course you did. You seem to have this all worked out. Why are you even talking to me? Why didn't you just bring Marie up here?"

"We need you to talk to her." Simon pursed his lips. "You know how sensitive she is about loyalty and I know she won't do it unless you let her know it's okay."

Van couldn't help it—he howled with laughter. "Oh, sure, you want me to convince her to leave me in the lurch? Sure. I'll get right on it."

"Van this could be huge for Marie and from what I saw downstairs—"

Van felt a hot and cold chill roll over his body. It would be good for Marie. It would be great for Marie, but they were a team. He wouldn't do it if they had offered this to him. Absolutely not. Well…he was pretty sure he wouldn't.

If you cared about her half as much as you care for

yourself you'd tell her to do it. You'd find her and tell her to go right ahead and be a huge star and leave you on AMSF with Pets That Look Like Their Owners.

He put the brakes on that kind of thinking. The only thing he knew for sure was that if she left *Adventures in Food*, his career would stall. He wasn't even sure what he felt for her and he was even more clueless about how she felt about him. He didn't need to sacrifice anything for love if nobody was in love.

This was a business decision and nothing else.

But as soon as he thought it, he felt sick to his stomach.

Love and business are an unfortunate combination.

"I'm going to pretend like this meeting never happened," Van said, turning for the door, wanting to walk far away from all of this.

"We're going to ask her anyway, Van," Simon said calmly. "We just wanted to give you a chance to discuss it with her. Come to a reasonable compromise."

"Screw you, Simon. Screw you and your compromises." Van slammed the door shut behind him, feeling both righteous and wrong at the same time. And neither sat well with him.

He wished he could pretend that the conversation never happened. But he couldn't. He went back to the restaurant and all he could think about was Marie and Food TV.

She came over to his condo that night. He sat

with her head in his lap while they watched a movie and ate popcorn, and he died a million deaths thinking about the show.

"Marie," he finally said when the credits rolled on the foreign film she had picked and he hadn't paid any attention to.

"Hmm?" She rolled onto her back and put her arms over her head.

She's so lovely. She's so lovely and if I tell her she could leave. He knew he was grasping at excuses, but in the end it didn't matter. He didn't tell her. They made love on the couch and afterward he stared up at the ceiling telling himself it was all right. He would tell her tomorrow. Over breakfast.

But of course he didn't.

For the next few days he fought with himself over whether to tell Marie about the plans Simon was making.

Saturday night, before they filmed the Pig Roast episode, Van climbed the stairs to her apartment after he had shut down Sauvignon. The door was unlocked like she told him it would be and he found her asleep in bed, a pool of moonlight highlighting her skin.

She was gorgeous, and just looking at her made him feel things he thought people like Mitch only made up. He watched as she shifted, her eyes fluttering open.

"Van?" Marie whispered, her eyes sleepy and her voice a croak. She ran a hand across her chin and he knew she was checking for drool. She was a drooler. He knew that, too. He also knew she slept on her right side and that she made dairy orders in her sleep. She loved mushrooms but they gave her gas. She cried during reruns of *M*A*S*H*. She loved kung fu movies, but closed her eyes during the violent parts. She gave the guy on the corner who begged for change a quarter and a sack of leftover scones every other day.

Van knew that she made him feel things that he never felt before.

Suddenly the tightness in his chest disappeared, the ball of tension and nerves he had been carrying in his stomach were gone.

I love her. He laughed, amazed, and suddenly what he needed to do became crystal clear.

"I'm going to turn on the light, okay?" he asked in a low voice and then flipped the switch on the lamp that sat on her bedside table.

"What's wrong?" she asked and moved over so he could sit beside her. He kissed the crease of worry that appeared between her eyes and for a brief moment he wondered if this conversation was going to be the beginning of the end for them. He wondered if by telling her about Food TV and then urging her to take it, if he would be losing the best thing that ever happened to him.

"Van? What's going on?" she asked. Marie sat up against the headboard.

"We need to talk." He took a deep breath, said

a quick prayer and started. "You know that blond guy that's been hanging around the sets the past few weeks?"

"Yeah?"

"Well, his name is Eric Maxwell and he is a producer for Food TV." She looked blank and then confused.

"How do you know?"

"I ah…Simon introduced me to him."

She shook her head and pushed her hair off her face. "What does he want?"

"He's interested in our show for Food TV."

"Our show?" she whispered but then her voice started climbing and Van winced. "You're having meetings with Simon and a producer for Food TV about our show without me! Van! That's a secret meeting and we agreed—"

"Listen." He had to stop her because she was beginning to shriek and jump to the wrong conclusion. "Food TV wants our show. A national show. They want it." There was a lump in his throat and he swallowed it, and recognized it was his pride. Mitch was right—everything comes at a price. "But they only want one of us to host it."

He saw it register on her face, a sudden dark anger and hurt, and he realized he was blowing it. "No, no, no. They want you, not me." Her mouth fell open and he had to smile even while it felt like he was tearing out part of his body. He touched her hair, the soft skin of her cheek. "I think you should do it."

"Food TV wants me to host our show alone?"

"Well, our show without the 'our,'" he agreed.

"Why did he go to you first?" she asked, confused and distrustful. His heart took another hit.

"Well, they actually went to Simon first and offered him a job as a producer and because he knows how loyal you are, he and Eric wanted me to tell you it was okay. It's okay, I mean that." He leaned in to kiss her, but she dodged the kiss.

"How long have you known?" He knew he couldn't blame her, this he did screw up, but it still stung that she didn't trust him.

"A week, since the Iron Chef taping. I know I should have told you, I meant to, at least a million times—"

"But you didn't," she whispered.

"No." He nodded his head. "I didn't and Marie, believe me when I say I am so sorry."

"But why not just tell me?"

"Because I am terrified that you're going to take it," he breathed. "Because my feelings were hurt that they didn't want me. Because I think you should go and do it and I don't want to lose you."

I love you, he thought but didn't say. It was baby steps with Marie and they were a million baby steps away from any sort of declaration of love. Though, looking at her, his heart was screaming it.

"I'm sorry I didn't tell you. I should have and I made a mistake."

There was a minute of silence that felt like an eon, while they both watched Marie pleat and unpleat the sheet in her hands. Van developed an ulcer waiting for her to say something.

"Marie—"

"We're a team," she said at the same time and then looked him in the eye, a small smile curving her mouth. "I'm not going to do it."

His heart leapt. *There you go, there's your answer, just leave it at that, man,* but he loved her and he had already taken the easy way out. He felt guilty and his conscience pushed him to get her to see reason and take the opportunity.

"A week ago, a day ago, maybe ten minutes ago I would have said 'Right! Screw 'em.'" He curved a hand over her shoulder. "But you've got to think about it, this is a whole lot bigger than…"

She cupped his face, and sat up until their mouths were a breath a part. "I won't do it, Van. I don't want it."

"Now you're lying. Of course you want this." He threw out his arms. "I want this."

She dropped her hands from his face and the suspicion was back in her eyes. "If I don't do it, are you going to take it?" she asked and even before the words were out of her mouth, he grabbed her shoulders.

"No," he said firmly. "You're right, we're a team."

Maybe it was because he caught her while she was sleeping, so all her armor was out of reach, but he could see everything she was feeling in her face and eyes. She didn't trust him.

"You don't believe me?" he asked, hurt. "I know I should have told you earlier, but Marie, I don't want that show any more than you do."

"I believe you," she told him. "I do." She was lying. He could tell, he could also tell that she wanted to believe in him. It wasn't much, but he would take it. He had taken a few leaps backward with her and it was going to take a lot of baby steps to win her faith back.

"WHY DON'T I SEE A PIG ROASTING on a fire?" Van asked. Marie yawned and pulled her hand away from Van's neck where she had been twirling strands of his hair in her fingers. He had hair like silk, and Marie had a hard time keeping her hands out of it. A woman would kill for his hair.

"Relax, Van." She patted his shoulder, recognizing the first signs of a freak-out.

Van parked and they got out of his car and crossed the street toward the parking lot of the Mission Dolores in the heart of the Mission District.

Van was right—there was no pig. Instead there was a giant black pot over a small **fire** in the middle of the asphalt parking lot. She subtly sniffed the air.

For this authentic Mexican pig roast, Marie had enlisted the help of her high-school friend Louisa Mancilla and Louisa's mother, Ruby. Ruby was one of the best cooks Marie had ever known. Marie had spent many nights at Ruby's kitchen table in raptures over mole sauce and homemade tamales.

Agnes came running up to them, her face set in firm but grave lines. "Okay, no freaking…"

"Great," Van threw his hands up in the air and glared at Agnes. "Now, I'm freaking."

"*Hola hola hola!*" Ruby Mancilla approached them, wiping her hands on the apron around her stout waist. She clutched Marie's face in her cold, damp hands and kissed her cheeks, and then did the same to Van. "*Buenas noches, Van. Buenas noches.*"

"What's in the pot, Ruby?" Van asked without preamble. Marie nodded, backing up her paranoid lover.

"Oh, Van, a surprise for you." Ruby turned her dancing brown eyes on Marie. "We love your show. Love it. You two…*muy caliente.*"

"Yeah, what's in the pot, Ruby?"

"Come see, Marie!" Louisa, her old friend, shouted from where she stood stirring the pot. Steam wreathed Louisa's head and the scent of heat, of peppers and spice filled the air. Marie's stomach growled.

She shot a glance at Van and he shrugged. "After you," he muttered and she let Ruby lead her over to the pot.

"We watch the show and we thought, a pig

roast would be so boring, what's interesting about roasted pork? Everyone eats *carnitas*."

"Well, not the snout," Van muttered. "We were going to eat the snout."

"Ah." Ruby made a face of distaste. "Pig snout is so beneath your show."

"So you changed the menu?" Marie asked, suddenly catching on the air the scent of singed fur and other unmistakable odors that had her shooting unbelieving looks at Ruby. *"No, Ruby, no you didn't..."*

Ruby laughed and laughed, and Marie and Van looked over the edge of the pot while Louisa stirred the tomato broth with herbs, onions and huge chunks of garlic.

"That doesn't look too—" Van started.

The goat head floated up to the surface.

"Goat-head soup!" Ruby said with flourish and pride.

"No!" Van shouted. "Absolutely not! Someone get a pig!"

"Just a moment, Ruby, excuse us." She led Van to the side before he could offend the easily offended Ruby.

"Marie! What the hell is going on?"

"They thought this would be funnier."

"Funnier? Goat head is funnier?" Van looked truly horrified and Marie couldn't blame him. You wake up one morning and people think it would be funny for you to eat the head of a goat. In a soup. It was a strange moment for anyone.

"Well, in our show I think it is."

Agnes joined their circle. The little blond man, Eric Maxwell, followed, though he stood a few feet behind her. Marie decided to take matters with Food TV into her own hands.

"Excuse me," she said to Agnes and Van. Van pulled on her hand and she turned back, knowing what he was going to say even before he said it.

"Marie, tell him you'll think about it."

"I don't want it." She shrugged and kissed his cheek before walking up to Eric Maxwell. He was a tiny man and tiny men as a rule made Marie nervous, mostly because they made her feel like an Amazon monster.

"Hi, Marie." He looked startled to see her approach him, but he tried to cover it. He held out his hand and Marie shook it.

"Van told me about the show and I'm not doing it without him," Marie said. "So unless you've changed the format, I don't think you need to keep coming around the sets. It's just a waste of time."

He smiled. "I like a woman who cuts to the chase." Marie tried not to cringe. *This guy is oilier than Simon.* "Please just give me chance to tell you about our offer."

"Eric, we're about to shoot and I'm not going to—"

"It's a great idea for a show," Eric interrupted. "We've got a sizeable budget and we would be sending you around the world so that you could find…" Marie couldn't do it. She couldn't listen to the details of what could be. She was foolish at times, but she wasn't going to be dumb. She knew she was doing the right thing saying no to Food TV, but a few months ago she would have jumped all over this.

"Listen, I really appreciate this, but I signed a contract…." Marie shrugged.

"This show wouldn't start until after your contract is up with *AMSF*."

"What about Van?" she asked.

Eric bit his lip and shrugged. "We've got male chefs all over the channel. We need another guy traipsing around the world like we need another roasted chicken recipe. We need a woman."

"Well, you'll have to find another woman."

"I think you have to ask yourself how much are you ready to sacrifice for Van."

Warning bells sounded in her head. Sacrificing things for a man wasn't something she had a lot of luck with. But, she couldn't live in the past forever.

Trust isn't something that just happens, you have to practice it, she told herself. She wanted to believe Van; surely that had to count for something.

She loved *AMSF*; her cooking empire was just the right size for her. Cozy but spacious with lots of room to grow. For the first time in two years, she was happy to be exactly where she was. "Staying at *AMSF* isn't a sacrifice. I am very happy."

"This opportunity might not come again."

"I don't expect it to," she told him honestly.

Eric sighed, letting his head fall down to his chest. Defeated. Marie almost felt bad for the guy.

"I'm going to leave you my card," he said, handing her the white card with the green Food TV logo. "Call me if you change your mind."

She took the card, but her mind was made up. Eric walked away and she could feel Van approach her from behind. Her skin, her whole body knew he was there before his hand even touched her neck.

"You didn't say no, did you?" he asked and she turned.

"I said no."

"Marie—"

"I don't want to work with that guy. I am really happy with the way things are right now."

"Okay," Van sighed, "but I think you're nuts."

"That's well established," she said with a smile and stood up on tiptoe to kiss him, determined to shove all of her doubts away.

"Ah, come on you guys, can we cut the crap and eat the soup?" Agnes muttered, pushing past them back toward the pot. "All right people. We need lights on that goat head."

14

TUESDAY MORNING Marie was running late. Pete had a problem with wild blueberry sour-cream coffeecake and she had stuck around to help him with the second try. She was carrying containers of her kid-friendly macaroni and apple slices with toffee that needed to be heated up before the segment started.

She would have liked a few minutes alone with Van to hug him and smell him and kiss his lips and find out what he had made for the kids. They had already gone over the script a few days ago, but neither of them had made any final decisions about what food they were making.

But she wanted to have a few words with Simon about his secret meetings.

She dropped the containers off with Agnes, gave her explicit directions for heating up the macaroni and cheese and ran up to Simon's office.

Simon's office was directly across from the stairwell, down a hallway, so that when Marie got to the top stair she could see the back of Van's head in the chair across from Simon's desk.

Her heart leaped and then sank. There was every chance that Van just stopped in Simon's office, just like she was about to. But her dubious heart lurched. *Maybe it's not a secret meeting, Marie. Give the guy a chance.* She saw Simon's hand waving around and as she approached, she could hear the loud rumble of their voices.

"Marie won't do it," she heard Van say and Marie stopped in her tracks. "She's out of the picture."

"Right, which is why we think you'll like this." Simon's hand picked up a poster-size piece of paper and turned it to Van. Marie, struck dumb in the hallway, saw it, too.

It was a poster for a Food TV show with Van's picture all over it.

"You've really outdone yourself, Simon," Van said and took the poster in his hands.

"I think this is a win/win situation for all of us." The final voice was Eric Maxwell's.

There was an awful buzzing in her ears. She had to work to breathe, to stay standing. *Get out of the hallway,* she told herself. *Walk. Get out before they see you.*

She turned and made it down the stairs on legs that wobbled. Anger at Van for lying to her and at herself for being the same fool twice in her life choked her.

She wandered through wardrobe and found a dark corner. Marie rested her forehead against the cool cement wall and Van's words echoed in her head.

Marie's out of the picture.

She picked up her head and bounced it against the wall. *You idiot. You dumb little girl. Twice? This has to happen to you twice before you get the message?*

Well, Marie got it this time. She got it loud and clear.

VAN LEFT SIMON'S OFFICE in a rage. The man had a lot of nerve. He hoped whomever they got to replace Simon as producer of *Adventures in Food* would be someone with a little more class. Someone with a better sense of loyalty. He shook his head walking through backstage, looking for Marie.

"Van, you've got ten minutes," Agnes said. "Whatever it is you made is warmed up in the wok on the stove."

"Great. Have you seen Marie?" he asked after her.

"She's onset, finishing her food."

He wished he had more time with her so they could have a laugh over the awful poster Simon had shown him. Apparently Simon's job at Food TV hinged pretty heavily on him getting the star for the show, which explained the song-and-dance number Van had gotten this morning—and had turned down in no uncertain terms.

Any doubt Van had had about him and Marie, about whether he would take the show if it were offered to him, was destroyed the day of the goat soup. She trusted him and he knew that was a gift far more important than Food TV.

But instead of time alone with Marie, he was going to have a half hour with three kids and his pretty damn brilliant kid-friendly recipes.

Those kids weren't going to know what hit them once they tried his sweet-and-sour meatballs with lo mein noodles and Chinese vegetables. It was colorful, it was well balanced and it was gourmet. In a word, perfect. He'd like to see Marie top that.

"Hey." He bounded up behind her on their dark stage. "I've missed you." He bent to kiss her neck, but she dodged out of the way. She turned and looked at him with eyes so flat and angry he took a step back. "Marie? What's wrong?"

She laughed once. A harsh bark. "You're good, Van. Very, very good."

"What are you talking about?"

"Hey, guys." Agnes came up to the set with three kids in tow. "I want you to meet Adam, Becky and Dakota." Van watched in horror as three kids pulled themselves up onto the bar stools across the counter from him and Marie. They sat there blinking like baby birds.

"Now's not the best time, Agnes," Van started. He could feel the animosity pouring off Marie.

"Well, now's the only time. You're on in five." Agnes left and the kids blinked.

Crap!

"Marie, I don't know what you're upset about but—"

"I think it would be best if you didn't talk to me right now." Marie pulled a casserole dish out of the oven. She pulled off the tinfoil covering it and ducked away from the steam that billowed up.

Van smelled pungent blue cheese. "You made macaroni and cheese with blue cheese for kids? It's gray!" He immediately wished he'd kept his mouth shut when Marie turned murderous eyes on him.

"We're on in three!" Agnes said.

"Marie," Van whispered, wondering what had happened. He saw her two days ago, talked to her yesterday and everything had been fine. "What's wrong?"

She ignored him and started plating her food.

"Are you ready for this show?" he asked, beginning to feel nervous. He didn't need this right before a live taping; he was still a bit stupid in front of those lights. He needed her, *they* needed her to be on top of her game.

Van heard *AMSF* go on commercial break, and he knew when they came back from break it was the *Adventures in Food* segment. He quickly stirred what was in the wok, barely tasted things and started plating his own food.

It will be okay, Marie will pull it together and we will be okay. He hoped, he really hoped.

Ten minutes later, Van was convinced he would

rather poke a dull stick in his eye than be on the stage with Marie and the three children from hell. Marie barely sounded human during her bit about the importance of nutrition for kids. He tried to make some joke and she just flat out pretended he hadn't said anything.

And the kids! Oh, God.

"It's pink." Adam, the eleven-year-old boy on the panel with spiky hair and early adolescent acne, curled up his lip at Van's meatballs. "I don't eat pink food."

"What is this?" Becky, a nine-year-old girl in pigtails pulled so tight it was amazing her scalp was not ripped open, held up a forkful of Van's lovely green vegetables.

"It's called bok choy," Van told them in an overly loud and overly slow voice.

"They're kids, not Japanese tourists," Marie muttered under her breath, but her mic picked it up. The studio audience laughed uncomfortably and Van was sure the strange energy between him and Marie was filling the entire building.

"Sweetheart, you made gray food. Excuse me if I don't take your advice on how to deal with children," Van snapped and the crowd was silent.

Marie shrugged and stood back with the same pained expression on her face. *She's throwing me to the dogs,* he thought and looked back at Adam, Becky and Dakota.

"It's very good for you," Van told the little girl,

who probably had never come within twenty feet of bok choy in her life.

"It looks gross." Her face twisted and she flung the bright green vegetable off her plate.

"Hey," Van admonished, "that's no way to behave."

"It's good!" the littlest girl, Dakota—a little chub in pink overalls whose face was now covered in sweet-and-sour sauce and blue cheese cream sauce—shouted.

Van turned smiling eyes on the seven-year-old until she had the gall to pick up one of Van's meatballs and roll it in Marie's macaroni sauce. She took the gooey mess and put it all in her mouth. "I like it!" she told everyone, spraying the table with food.

"No, you're not supposed to eat them together, you're supposed to eat them separately." Van quickly pulled Marie's plate away from the little garbage disposal.

Marie chuckled into her dishtowel and Van bit his tongue. She had better have a good explanation for acting this way.

"This is good," Becky said brightly, dipping one of the apple slices into the small dish of warmed caramel toffee that Marie had prepared.

"That's dessert," Van cried. He pulled that away from the girl and now his arms were filled with dishes of food. "Let's try all of this again," he said and shot Marie a desperate look.

Please Marie work with me, we're dying here.

"Cue commercial," Agnes whispered to Mike.

Marie managed to get them out to commercial and when the red lights came off the cameras, he turned on her, fed up.

"Can you help me?" Van snapped at Marie. Their eyes met and he had no clue what was going on in her head. "I will talk about whatever has pissed you off in about twenty-two minutes. Until then—" he jerked his thumb at the two prepubescent monsters and one walking garbage disposal "—can we just get through this?"

Marie looked like she was biting her tongue, and then she finally turned toward the kids. "Listen up!"

"Who are you, lady?" Adam said, sneering.

"I want my mom," Becky cried, pushing away the food. "I don't want to eat this stuff."

Marie leaned over the counter and got in the faces of the three kids. "I will pay you each ten dollars to eat this food. You don't have to like it. You can make faces and say it's dog poo—"

"You said poo—" Dakota laughed into her food-covered hands.

Marie shook her head, focusing on the other two. "All right? Ten bucks."

"Twenty," Adam negotiated and Van had to give the kid points for balls.

"Twenty it is." She shook their hands and leaned back, standing next to Van at the counter.

Van leaned into her. "We need to talk," he said.

"You bet your ass we do," she practically hissed and Van again was left to wonder what was wrong.

"We've got ten." Agnes yelled and before Van was really ready, the red lights were on again and Marie was finally back with the living, running the rest of the segment like a scary cross between a kindergarten teacher and a drill sergeant.

"It tastes like poo!" Dakota shouted, smiling and clapping her hands.

"Yeah," Becky agreed, nibbling the tiniest corner of the bok choy. "It's gross."

"The noodles aren't bad," Adam grumbled, staring at his plate.

"Ah, success," Van said into the eye of the camera.

MARIE HAD RUN after the segment was over. It was chickenshit, she knew that, but she had to get a grip on her hurt. She wanted to bawl and scream and ask him how he could do this to her when she had given it up for him. And those were the last things she needed to do. She needed a cool head and emotional detachment. So she ran for the bathroom and didn't come out until she felt like she had a grip.

She couldn't find him anywhere until a young tech guy told her Van had bummed a cigarette and went outside to smoke it. She recognized the guy from after the planning meeting they had had two and a half months ago. It felt like years.

She went out the side door and nearly ran into Van.

"What the hell was wrong with you in there?" he asked, dropping the cigarette and stepping on it. Marie was glad he was mad; she wanted a good fight.

"How long were you planning on keeping it from me, Van?" she snapped. She tossed her black hair from her shoulders and her eyes sent off sparks.

"Keep what from you?"

"Stop pretending!" she yelled and Van stepped back. *Good*, she thought, *you better take cover.* "Don't treat me like an idiot anymore."

"Wait a second, I never treated you like an idiot."

"Oh." She opened her eyes wide and let all her anger drip like venom. "You weren't treating me like an idiot when you were telling me to take the Food TV show one minute and the next minute you were taking it?"

He shook his head, baffled. "I'm not taking the—"

She made a low angry sound of frustration and fisted her hands in her hair. "Stop lying to me, Van. Stop it. I saw you."

"Saw me? Marie, honest to God, I…" He reached out for her and she slapped his hands away.

"This morning, Van. This morning. Simon showed you the poster. Surely you must remember?"

It took him a second and Marie wondered if

maybe she hadn't been sleeping with the best, un-discovered acting talent in the world. But then he laughed and she felt like she had been slapped. *Oh God, I was such a fool.* His big booming laugh broke her anger and the hurt flooded through the cracks. She took off for her car.

"Marie, Marie." He ran after her, getting in front of her so she had to stop. "They were desper-ate after you said no and they asked their second choice." He pointed to himself. "Me."

"Well congratulations, Van, second choice is better than nothing." She took off again and Van grabbed her arm. She turned, jerking her arm away, hating the touch of him.

"I said no, for the same reasons you did Marie. We're a team."

"You said no?"

"I said no."

She tested herself, pulled against the ties that bound her to her lonely place in the past, but it didn't work. She searched herself but she couldn't find any trust, any faith. It was all gone. She looked up at the sky, furiously blinking back tears. The man she was half-convinced she was in love with was obviously telling her the truth and she still couldn't trust him.

I am so damaged, she thought. She was wrecked beyond repair.

"Do you believe me?" he asked, taking a careful step toward her. When she looked back at him he was blurred by the tears standing in her eyes. She couldn't speak past the lump of anger and sorrow in her throat.

"You don't trust me?" He was hurt, she had hurt him and she could barely breathe because of it.

He reached out to touch her and she shied away. "Don't," she breathed. She squared her shoulders. "I don't trust anyone, Van. It's just the way it is."

That's not true, a voice buried deep in her heart called out. *Give yourself a chance, Marie. Give Van a chance.* But she squelched that voice with the cold, hard facts of her miserable track record.

"Marie, I'm not doing the show. I swear." Van reached out for her again, but then dropped his hands. "Let's go someplace else so we can talk."

It was on the tip of her tongue to say okay. To sit with him and talk to him and try to believe in the best of herself, that she could get over the past. She could have a few more days, maybe weeks, a month at the most, of sleeping next to him, but what would be the point? She knew she would just be prolonging the inevitable. If it didn't end now, it would end later.

"Van, it's..." She took a breath. "It's over. All of it's over." She slung her bag over her shoulder. "We can be business partners or we can be lovers, but we can't be both."

"Marie, come on, let's talk." Van was white and

his black eyes held a world of hurt, fresh and new, and she had to get away.

"There's nothing to talk about, Van." She forced herself to be cool, distant. "You said you wanted to be my lover more than my friend and—" she swallowed "—I'm telling you I want to be business partners more than lovers."

"Marie, you told me about Ian." His voice was anguished and her head snapped toward him when he said Ian's name. "You told me your secrets—that has to count for something."

She remained silent, seething in the quiet, afraid of what might come pouring out of her if she opened her mouth. "I thought it did."

She couldn't help it, her fingers came up to her bracelets. Her little touchstones for the mistakes she had made in her life. Suddenly Van was furious. He grabbed her shoulders and she let him, surprised to see him so angry. "You need to get rid of those bracelets. You can't think of the future because those damn things keep you in the past."

"Don't tell me—"

"Five mistakes that you won't forget about? Ian abandoning you is not a mistake of yours. And you don't trust me right now because of some guy who screwed you in the past! I am not Ian."

"Every guy in one way or another is Ian, Van!" she shouted back at him. "Some more than others.

So you didn't take the job this time. What about next time? Am I really supposed to believe that you would sacrifice—" she stumbled over that word "—you would sacrifice a bigger and better career for a woman you're sleeping with?"

He was quiet for so long, staring at her with sad and solemn eyes that she guessed she won. She had come up with the argument he couldn't fight. She straightened her shoulders and took a step away from him.

"I love you, Marie, I love you. I love everything about you."

Marie felt her heart stop, her whole body started trembling. *Leave*, she ordered her body. *Run. Go. Don't listen to this.* But she couldn't move.

"I love your talent and your pride and your intelligence and your loyalty. I love your belly and the things you make me feel and—"

"Stop," she whispered, tears falling down her cheeks. This was the cruelest trick. The words she so badly wanted to hear and she couldn't let herself believe them.

She didn't trust him. What was the point?

Marie threw her hair over her shoulder and gathered all of her pride. "Now, I really don't believe you. It's over, Van. We're done. You should take the Food TV job." She pulled her hands away and Van let her go.

She walked past him and left him in that parking lot with her head held high, thinking she was doing the right thing. But she couldn't shake the fear that she was walking away from her one true shot at happiness.

15

MARIE IGNORED HIS CALLS. She ignored the flowers. Mitch Palyard even called, inviting her to dinner at his home and she managed to say no to that, because she didn't believe him when he promised Van wouldn't be there. It broke her heart, but she did it.

AMSF made the official announcement that after the last episode, Simon would be leaving. He didn't get the Food TV job because neither Van nor Marie would take the show, so he was going to a Los Angeles affiliate. Agnes got promoted to Simon's job, and Marie and Van were offered a two-year deal at *AMSF* for *Adventures in Food.*

Marie stared at the ceiling every night, for four nights, wishing there was a saxophone keeping her awake rather than the pain that was crushing her chest. Saturday night, a night that she would have spent with Van after he closed the restaurant, she wondered, stupidly, what Van was doing. If he was all right.

Marie shut her eyes. Breaking up with Van had

nothing to do with business and had everything to do with her own insanity. Something wasn't right in her. Something got screwed up a long time ago, before Ian, before Van. She could probably pay someone a fortune to find out that it was all her mother's fault.

She guessed there was a good chance she was wrong, that they could manage a work-and-personal relationship. That she could grow to trust him, to trust in something other than herself. But every time she thought about calling him and apologizing and begging him to try it again, all she had to do was touch her bracelets and it all came back to her. The pain and hurt, the humiliation and sacrifice.

You've got to take care of yourself, because no one else is going to do it. They were cold words to live by.

She curled herself up on her side and pressed her nose into the pillow Van used to use. The smell was almost gone. In a few days' time it would be like he had never been there at all.

THE SUNDAY THAT MARIE and Van were supposed to review each other's restaurants, Marie got the two-year contracts from Agnes. Marie had no time to look at them, so she shoved them in her bag on the way to the shoot.

Marie did the review of Van's place with her tongue firmly in her cheek. She wanted to flood the room with light and make fun of the pink walls, but she thought about how chagrined he was by them. The strong, stubborn, resolute man would take the jokes on the chin, but he would be privately hurt that she would make fun of it. So she kept the lights low.

At the same time, she wanted to kiss the pink walls, hug every single thing that Van might have touched.

She sat at the bar and ate what the waiter brought her—mini portions of perfectly prepared filet and pasta and oven-baked pizzas. She drank the small half pints of exotic foreign beer that the bartender poured for her to drink with every small meal.

"How is everything so far?" Dave, the bartender, asked, leaning his elbows on the bar next to her. Van used to do the same thing.

"It's fantastic," Marie said past the lump in her throat. "Really awesome."

"He's behind you," Dave whispered. "Behind the lights. I don't know what you did, Marie, but the guy is going off the deep end."

Marie whirled before she thought better of it. In the darkness behind the bright lights she saw Van, tall and large with his arms crossed over his chest and his legs braced wide.

He lifted his hand in a wave and then vanished.

It's for the best, Marie, the adult voice told her, and Marie turned back to the bar and focused with all of her strength on taking care of herself.

ANNA STARTED her maternity leave a month before her due date. She told Marie it was to get ready for the baby, but Sam said she hadn't done much except lie on the couch and eat, and then talk about how big she was getting.

It didn't sound that different from Marie's life. All she did was lie in bed, think about Van and tell herself not to think about Van.

Tuesday morning, Marie brought over breakfast for Anna and Sam so they could all watch *Adventures in Food* together.

"I am so glad you're here," Sam said, meeting her at the door. "I love her, but I might kill her before this baby is born."

Marie kissed her handsome brother-in-law on the cheek and handed off the containers of food.

"Please tell me there is something fried or covered in cheese in one of those containers?" Anna called out from her position on the couch.

"I'm going to go put these things away," Sam said, beating a quick retreat to the kitchen. Marie kicked off her shoes in the foyer and padded across the gorgeous hardwood floors into the living room, where Anna was doing her beached-whale impression on one of their new deep red twill couches.

"Hey, sis." Anna said, struggling to sit up, but Marie waved her back down.

"Stay comfortable, Anna," she said. She kissed Anna's cheek and looked around. It had been a while since she had been in Anna and Sam's house. Last time it hadn't been finished, but now all the walls were painted, pictures were up, books sat on shelves.

The house looked great. It looked like a home.

"I like the pictures, Anna." Marie crossed the room to the wall filled with photos of Sam and Anna and family. Well, Sam's family. She and Anna just had each other. Marie painfully realized that wasn't really true anymore. Anna had Sam and Sam's family, and soon this baby. Marie was growing more and more periphery to Anna's life.

"Thanks, they're not nearly as dramatic as yours, but Sam doesn't understand pictures without people in them."

Marie took a deep breath that shuddered a little in her chest. She barely had any photos with people in them, and standing in front of a wall of goofy snapshots of people she didn't know, she felt terribly alone.

"Hey, when do you guys go on?" Sam asked coming back into the room with plates of the fruit and cheese she had brought. He set one of the plates down on Anna's stomach and then lifted her feet so he could sit under them.

Marie checked her watch. "We're on in about five minutes." Sam grabbed the remote and turned the volume up.

Marie wanted to pretend she didn't care. Not so much about Van reviewing her restaurant, or even seeing herself on TV, which had always been kind of thrilling. She tried to pretend that she didn't want to see him or hear his voice.

Anna and Sam laughed at all the jokes she made about Van being stuffy, and his food and restaurant being old-fashioned, but delectable.

Van came on the screen walking through her restaurant with authority, dressed in black, and Marie couldn't swallow.

She didn't listen to what he was saying, so engrossed was she in seeing him. She remembered how she used to think he wasn't handsome. She shook her head at her own foolish pride. He was gorgeous and, for a brief minute, he had been hers. *What have I done?* she wondered.

The camera on Van panned up to her painted ceiling and Anna laughed.

"What? What'd he say?" Marie asked, not turning away from the screen.

The camera panned back down and there was Van with his half grin. He pointed up to the ceiling and the cuff of his black chef jacket slid down his arm, and there at his wrist was a silver bracelet.

"Now that is fussy," Van said onscreen, obviously joking, but Marie only heard him through a vacuum. His sleeve got caught on the bracelet, leaving it exposed.

Marie couldn't breathe. She was scarring Van like she had been scarred, leaving him a silver bracelet as a reminder of the kind of pain that was in this world if you weren't careful.

I did that, she thought, and all she wanted to do was take that pain away. Pride, career, independence, nothing mattered as much as the wild want she had to take it all back.

"I've made a terrible mistake," she moaned, putting her head in her hands.

"What have you done?" Anna asked. Marie turned in time to see Sam push her sister upright by the butt.

"I broke up with Van."

"What? Why?" Anna asked, her brow knit. She and Sam shared a concerned look.

"Because I am stupid." She flopped down in the chair. The tears she had been fighting off for days welled back up in her eyes. But nothing could change what she knew to be true. "I need to take care of myself because no one is going to do that for me."

"No duh, Marie," Anna snapped. "Jeez, you'd think you would learn something with all the meddling you did in my life."

Marie turned startled eyes on Sam, who winced and shrugged. "You woke the beast," he whispered.

"You don't give anyone a chance to take care of you, Marie. You leave when people get close. You know, I am surprised you even started a relationship with Van."

"You and me both," Marie muttered.

"Because he's perfect for you." Anna just kept going, a pregnant steamroller. "You couldn't create a guy better for you and eventually you were going to have to dump him for some dumb reason and I was going to have to watch you try to pretend like you were all right." She threw her hands in the air. "Like right now. Well, I'm done Marie. You made a mistake. Big. Huge. And I am sorry I don't have the imagination to concoct some big ruse to get you to come to grips with it like you did for me, but trust me here little sister. You push that guy away and it will be nothing but old, alone Auntie Marie for my kids."

"Hey!" Marie cried. "That's a little harsh."

"Yeah, well, I'm a little pregnant." Anna maneuvered herself back into a sitting position and fanned her red face. Sam chuckled and patted his wife on the shoulder.

"She may lack a certain level of politeness, but Anna is right," Sam piped up and Marie rolled her eyes.

"Sam, I love you but I don't know if I can take any more honesty from anyone right now."

He shrugged. "That's fair. But let me just tell you as a guy whose heart was broken by one of the Simmons' girls, you aren't easy to love. You're gorgeous, but you're nuts. You are independent to a fault, you are so sure you're right all the time, sometimes you lie and you can be mean."

"Hey!" Marie butted in, offended.

"You should have just stopped at gorgeous," Anna whispered, stroking her husband's face.

Sam kissed Anna and continued. "I don't blame you. Your mother did quite a number on you guys as kids. But guys like me and Van, we're once in a lifetime for you girls. Most men aren't going to take on the dragons to find the princesses underneath. You think it's easy falling in love with you? Getting you to drop all that armor you two hold so dear? All that 'it's me against the world' bullshit you love." He glanced at his wife, "Sorry, Anna. Think again. You've shown him the real you and if he's still coming back for more, trust me, he loves you. And if you can't trust a guy who's put in all that work? Well, you're dumber than your sister was."

From one breath to the next, Marie's whole life opened up. She inhaled and felt the hard, dark kernel of hurt and anger that was wedged next to her heart crack open and dissolve. "I gotta go." She stood up and grabbed her bag.

"Leave the food," Anna insisted.

"There's pizza in the bottom container." She ran for the door, ran back and kissed her sister and Sam. "I love you. Both."

"Go get him," Anna cheered. "And bring him back here so we can threaten him if he ever hurts you."

"Just go get him," Sam amended.

Marie left, her heart a hundred yards ahead of her.

She parked her VW illegally in front of his condo, nearly running into Van's empty garbage cans that were lined up in front of the curb. It was 8:30 a.m., she wasn't even sure if Van would be up yet.

Better, that's better, she thought, imagining Van all rumpled and half-naked and surprised and glad to see her. She jumped out of her car, dodging the garbage cans.

She pounded hard on the door until she heard Van inside swearing. "Hey, I get the idea…." Van whipped open the door and stopped dead. "Marie."

Marie took him in, drank him in like water, like wine. He wore a black T-shirt with a hole in the collar, his hair was on end and he had a day's growth of beard clouding his face. He was so handsome, so attractive to her. He had called to her and she had been a fool trying to pretend not to hear.

"You've got a lot of nerve coming in here after the cracks you made about me being stuffy."

"Well, that's me, nervy."

He laughed once, a dry bark. Obviously, he disagreed.

"Sweetheart, you're the biggest chicken I've ever met." He gestured for her to come inside and as she walked past him, Marie decided that maybe bravado wasn't the way to go here.

"All right." She grabbed his hand, her fingers sliding over his wrist and hitting the silver bracelet he now wore. She took a deep breath, stepping way off the well-worn path of her usual behavior. She was stepping into uncharted territory. Honesty. Desperation.

"You're right, I'm a total coward," she admitted. She put one finger under the bracelet, laying the pad of her finger on his pulse point. "But I want to try…" she whispered. "It's just that I am so bad at it…."

Van looked down at her hand on his wrist and Marie felt good, felt true. He was going to give her a chance, he was going to let her make this right, but then he shook off her hand.

"Tea?" he asked casually, as if she were someone who hadn't slept in his arms, hadn't taken him in her body.

"No!" she cried. She shook her head, bounced on her toes, feeling like there was a swarm of angry bees in her chest. "Van. I love you," she said and grabbed his arms. "I know I've really screwed this up, but I love you and I'm sorry and I don't want to be business partners more than I want to be your lover. I want to be here, with you. I want…" Van's mouth fell open and he blinked at her. "Okay, okay." She nodded her head. "I can see I've shocked you or…I've…I really don't know what I've done. I don't really know what I'm doing." She was spitting on him in her wild effort to get all the words out at once. And he wasn't saying anything, which she didn't think was a good sign. He certainly wasn't sweeping her up in his arms, which is what she had hoped for after the "I love you" part.

She remembered the contracts that were still in her purse from Sunday. She stepped away from Van and fished them out. "Look, see, I can prove it. I trust you." She ripped the contract in half. "I believe in you." She ripped them again. "I love you and nothing else matters."

She tried to come up with words that would convey more, that would make what she was feeling make sense. But there were none, and she knew what she had to do.

"My mom kicked me out of the house when I was sixteen." She took off her oldest bracelets, one from each wrist and threw them on top of the torn up contract. Van looked like he was about to say something, but she talked over him. She was a rolling stone at this point, and it was best to stay out of her way. "Anna took me in, no questions asked." The second bracelets fell onto the contract. "I went to go find my father when I graduated high school and he told me I could stay with him if I wanted, but I left. And I should have stayed." With each bracelet Marie felt younger, lighter. She put her hand on the first of the fourth sets of bracelets and her mind drew a blank. She laughed; she'd been carrying this baggage so long she forgot what was in it. "I have no idea why I am wearing these." She shrugged and peeled off the last bracelet, Ian's bracelet. "And this is Ian's, and I don't care anymore. I am not holding on to this crap. I love you and I trust in you." The bracelet hit the ground and rolled against Van's foot, and Marie took a deep breath.

I am brand new, she thought.

He shook his head, stroked the scar on his chin and looked down at the contract and bracelets. "Well, there are things that definitely make more sense now. You expect me to run for the hills?" he asked.

"I wouldn't be surprised," she whispered.

"Marie, it's going to take more than a little baggage and some trust issues to scare me off."

Oh, she thought, *his eyes.* She could read them again. There he was, everything that made up Van, pride and skill and intelligence and humor and...his love for her. Marie began to cry and Van hauled her into his arms.

Oh, come on, show a little control here, would you? She tried to get a grip, but all of her distance and cynicism and fear were gone, and she was just a woman crying because a man she loved loved her back.

"What about your bracelet?" she asked, finding the silver with her fingers. "I thought you were going to never forgive me or let yourself make the same mistake."

"Well, Marie, I hate to burst your bubble, but this bracelet isn't about you," he told her archly.

"It's a reminder to not let my pride stand in the way of doing what's right. I should have told you the second Simon mentioned Food TV. There are things more important than me and my career." He pressed a kiss to her mouth.

Marie moaned and wrapped her arms around his neck. She kissed him, opened her mouth to him and felt as if she might just fall apart right there. How much could one person take?

"Speaking of careers..." He broke the kiss and looked down at the contract pieces they were standing on. "Was that your contract for *Adventures in Food?*"

She nodded.

"That might have been a tad dramatic." He pulled her a little tighter. "Maybe you can just sign mine."

"So, we're going to do this? Business partners and lovers?" she asked, her face pressed into his T-shirt, into his warm spicy smell.

"Yeah," he said. "I think we are. I think we can do it." Van's eyes narrowed. "For a while. And then I think we should be business partners, lovers and parents."

"Oh, no!" Marie moaned, laughing, but her heart soared. "After my blue-cheese cream sauce and your bok choy, you think we can do that?"

"Marie," Van said, shaking her a bit in his arms, "I think we can do anything."

Marie felt unfettered, loose and carefree, near

tears and near laughter at the same time. "So do I," she breathed.

"You know, I've got some great ideas for next season. I think we should do something with fondue and…"

Marie, because she was happy and in love, took off her shirt and threw it over her head. Van stopped talking.

"Keep going," she urged him on, toeing off her tennis shoes so she could take off her pants. "You were talking about fondue."

"Right." Van was obviously distracted by her breasts and the blue lace bra she was wearing, so she decided to give him a thrill. She took off the bra.

"You're talking about next season…." She unbuttoned the top button of her jeans.

"Right." Van's eyes were fixed on her pants. "I think we should really rethink the chicken recipes."

"Veto. No chicken recipes." Marie took off her pants and Van audibly swallowed.

"Marie, your body…" He smiled. "It's just not fair."

"Oh, Van." She grabbed the waist of his pants. "Haven't you figured it out yet?" She toyed with his zipper. "All's fair in love and war."

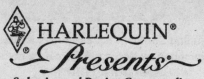

HARLEQUIN®
Presents

Seduction and Passion Guaranteed!

Introducing a brand-new trilogy by

Sharon Kendrick

Passion, power & privilege – the dynasty continues
with these handsome princes...

Welcome to Mardivino—a beautiful and wealthy
Mediterranean island principality, with a prestigious
and glamorous royal family. There are three
Cacciatore princes—Nicolo, Guido and
the eldest, the heir, Gianferro.

Next month (May 05), meet Nico in

THE MEDITERRANEAN
PRINCE'S PASSION #2466

Coming in June: Guido's story, in

THE PRINCE'S LOVE-CHILD #2472

Coming soon: Gianferro's story in

THE FUTURE KING'S BRIDE

Only from Harlequin Presents

Are you getting it at least twice a month?

Here's how: Try RED DRESS INK books on for size & receive two FREE gifts!

Bombshell
by Lynda Curnyn

As Seen on TV
by Sarah Mlynowski

YES! Send my two FREE books.
There's no risk and no purchase required—ever!

Please send me my two FREE tradesize paperback books and bill me just 99¢ for shipping and handling. I may keep the books and return the shipping statement marked "cancel." if I do not cancel, about a month later I will receive 2 additional books at the low price of just $11.00 each in the U.S. or $13.56 each in Canada, a savings of over 15% off the cover price (plus 50¢ shipping and handling per book*). I understand that accepting the two free books places me under no obligation ever to buy any books. I can always return a shipment and cancel at any time. Even if I never buy another book from Red Dress Ink, the free books are mine to keep forever.

160 HDN D367   360 HDN D37K

Name (PLEASE PRINT)

Address   Apt. #

City   State/Prov.   Zip/Postal Code

Want to try another series? Call 1-800-873-8635
or order online at www.TryRDI.com/free.

In the U.S. mail to: 3010 Walden Ave., P.O. Box 1867, Buffalo, NY 14240-1867
In Canada mail to: P.O. Box 609, Fort Erie, ON L2A 5X3

*Terms and prices subject to change without notice. Sales tax applicable in N.Y.
**Canadian residents will be charged applicable provincial taxes and GST.

All orders subject to approval. Offer limited to one per household.
® and ™ are trademarks owned and used by the trademark owner and/or its licensee.

© 2004 Harlequin Enterprises Ltd.

RED DRESS INK™

RDI04MMP

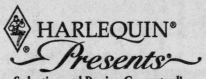

HARLEQUIN®
Presents

Seduction and Passion Guaranteed!

GREEK TYCOONS

They're the men who have everything—
except brides...

Wealth, power, charm—what else could a
heart-stoppingly handsome tycoon need?
In the GREEK TYCOONS miniseries you have
already been introduced to some gorgeous Greek
multimillionaires who are in need of wives.

**Now it's the turn of favorite Presents
author Lucy Monroe,
with her attention-grabbing romance**

THE GREEK'S INNOCENT VIRGIN
Coming in May
#2464

Be sure to catch your favorite
Harlequin Flipside authors
writing for other Silhouette
and Harlequin series!

SILHOUETTE *Romance* ®

Holly Jacobs
in Silhouette Romance

ONCE UPON A PRINCESS
May 2005

ONCE UPON A PRINCE
July 2005

ONCE UPON A KING
September 2005

Also watch for:

Stephanie Doyle in Silhouette Bombshell in July 2005

Elizabeth Bevarly, Cindi Myers and Dawn Atkins
appearing in Harlequin Blaze in Fall 2005

Stephanie Rowe writing for Harlequin Intrigue in 2006

Barbara Dunlop in Silhouette Desire in 2006

Look for books by these authors at your favorite retail outlet.